MURDER, COIN

ANOTHER D.S. JOHN ROSE INVESTIGATION

JAMES GLACHAN

SALTCOATS POLICE STATION
5TH AUGUST 2024 08:55

DETECTIVE SERGEANT John Rose returned to Saltcoats police station and, as he expected, the Cold Case team. When he walked into the station he wasn't in the best of moods, the first week in August and it was raining. Not a summery shower but a heavy outburst and more predicted for the rest of the day. It was more wintery than the end of summer. Winter depressed him.

The desk sergeant called him over and told him Detective Inspector Ross, his superior, wanted to see him first thing.

'Thanks, will do,' he answered but as ever didn't mean it. Instead, he went straight up to his office. Walking in he expected to see his assistant, D.C. Helen Begg.

He was shocked to find to find not only that she wasn't there, but another Detective Constable sat at his desk and one he didn't recognise.

He waited for the detective to turn round before he spoke.

For a second or ten he thought he had either opened the wrong office door or was in some twilight zone. It was neither, he obviously had been replaced.

'You must be D.S. Rose. The Detective Inspector wants to see you. Did they not tell you at the front desk?' he said before John got a word in.

John didn't speak. He simply turned and walked out letting the door swing closed behind him.

As he walked down the stairs he realised one thing for

certain, moves were afoot. He shook his head- uniform. He reckoned his bosses wanted him back in uniform to force him out early. They obviously hadn't taken his letter of resignation and 2 months notice well.

He had bad news for them if that was the route they wanted to go, he would rather go on the sick than let them think they had beaten him.

John looked through the glass of the Inspector's office. The D.I. was waiting for him and waved him in.

John walked in and sat down without speaking. Waiting.

'How did you find Ayr police station?' Michelle Ross asked.

'I used my Sat-nav, took me straight there.'

'Humour? Not like you John. Is this the new you because you have put your retiral notice in?'

Before he answered she went on, 'I was off on holiday when you came in with it. Surprised me a bit when I found out.'

'Surprised me too,' he said then went on, 'in answer to your question, no. I haven't suddenly found humour.' John had just said the first thing that came to mind when his boss had asked him about Ayr. He was just back from a spell being seconded to Ayr and had solved a murder case very quickly.

'Ayr was ok. The crew were good, that was why we got the job done quickly. Boss was hopeless, you know how inept male Detective Inspectors are. So, who is the new guy in my office and what does that mean for me?'

'Straight to the point as ever. Detective Constable Ballantine is my replacement for Helen Begg. He was doing cold cases in Ayr so it seemed the place to put him.'

John had been mentoring Helen for about 10 months, since she joined the detectives from uniform. She also had joined him in Ayr and told him she wanted to transfer there. He was surprised it had happened so quickly for her.

The Inspector paused after that. John waited for her to continue and answer the second part of his question, the bit about him.

Michelle held her pause, leaving John to break the silence.

'Helen told me she wanted to transfer from Saltcoats to Ayr, but it seems to me that her transfer's been very quick.'

'Oh, your quick result on the Miller case got you and the team a lot of Brownie points hence Ayr were desperate to keep her. Wanted to keep you too.'

'Okay, boss, let's stop beating about the bush, what is happening with me?' John asked.

'Your great skills have been requested in Kilmarnock.'

'Kilmarnock? Why Kilmarnock?'

'To quote one of your favourite sayings, above my pay grade that decision.'

'Doing what? I have only 2 months left before I stop?'

'You are needed to add your experience to the serious crime squad. Why, what did you think? You didn't think you were being busted back to uniform or something like that, did you?'

'What? No, I expected it to be serious crime.'

'Well, I must admit I will be sorry to see you go. I am sure we can get together for a drink before you stop.'

'When do I report to Kilmarnock?' he asked.

The Detective Inspector looked up at her office clock: 'About half an hour ago. You were supposed to be contacted last week.'

'Typical Saltcoats detective squad efficiently,' John said as he got up.

The 2 shook hands and John left, heading for his office. He travelled lightly but his special mug should be there.

He opened the office door without knocking. Ballantine looked round surprised.

'It's okay, don't get up,' John said. He looked around the desk and saw his mug was being used as a pencil and pen holder. John reached over and emptied the mug's contents all over the desk.

'My mug,' was all he said, showing its message to the stunned officer. The mug's simple message- If nobody else can solve it they send for papa.

'Have a nice career,' John said as he turned and left the office for good.

KILMARNOCK POLICE STATION 10:05

JOHN ARRIVED at Kilmarnock police station just after 10 o'clock. The woman officer at the front desk looked at him in a way that said- who are you and what do you want.

John answered her look. 'Detective Sergeant John Rose.'

Her look changed to one of- should that mean anything to me, it doesn't.

'I am here to join the serious crime squad.'

'Okay,' she said slowly. 'Have you been here before?'

'I was seconded here about 20 years ago, haven't been back since.'

'It's okay, it's still in the same place. Second floor, end of the corridor.'

She buzzed the lock on the door through to the staff only area. John took his warrant card out of his pocket and held it up for her to see.

'You should have checked this first,' he said, then turned and headed for the unlocked door. It wasn't like him to be bitchy, but the woman just caught him at a bad moment.

John walked up the stairs to the second floor. He stopped at the top landing just to check his breathing was okay, didn't want his first impression to be asthmatic looking. Then he walked down the corridor looking for the serious crime squad office.

The corridor ended in a glass door which had serious crime squad stencilled on the glass in capital letters.

He could see about 8 fellow detectives sitting behind desks studying their computer screens, and in the far corner there was a separate office, no doubt for the senior officer. It was occupied, although from the distance he couldn't see who was using it.

He let himself in and walked through the main office, heading for the boss. A few heads turned from their screens for a moment then back, but nobody thought to speak.

Turned out there was a woman sitting behind the boss's desk. Another woman, John felt a shudder down his spine. His last, what, 3 of the last 4 gaffers had been women and each not very good at their job's. Excepting his last boss, D.I. Ross. He was sorry to be leaving her. She knew what he could do and let him get on with it. The others tried to tell him how to do his job.

The woman waiting for him turned out to be Detective Inspector Chris Field who waved him in. John thought she was a bit younger, maybe 10 years, than his 64 and although going grey had been a redhead in her younger days.

'You must be Rose,' she said quite abruptly. In response he merely nodded as he sat down on the chair opposite her she waved him to take.

'Chris Field,' she said by way of introduction, 'but you can call me boss.'

John liked that, a woman, and a strong one at that, who laid the ground rules down from the start.

'People say I am a hard bitch, but the truth is I just don't suffer fools gladly. You be fair with me, and I will be fair with you. Cross me to your peril. I am down to bare bones with my squad. Sick leave, maternity and one in hospital.'

'Who are all those out there?'

'The total squad for the whole division. Anyway, as you have put your notice in it was decided you go back on the murder squad in general and here in particular, as I said, we are down to the bare bones.

Don't know how you feel about that, but the decision was made above my pay grade, and we need to live with that. The good news is I will be watching your every move until you leave.' She smiled as she said it.

Although retirement was only in 2 months' time, it

suddenly seemed to be a long way away to him.

'What do we have at the moment?' he asked, hoping for something to get going on.

'Nothing current. Just check the records there are up to date.' She said with a smile again. John reckoned his former bosses had forewarned anybody who was in charge of him that record keeping was his Achilles heel.

'Take the first desk on the left there. All the better for me to keep an eye on you.'

John left the office with a heavy heart, as far as he knew deaths in Kilmarnock were either domestic or junkies, though not necessarily in that order.

7TH AUGUST 2024 10:15
BAR XX KILMARNOCK

LYNNE MURDOCH sighed before she opened the front door to the bar but smiled as she walked into her bar. Bar XX on John Finnie Street in Kilmarnock was her baby but after a week in Tenerife it was a thousand miles away from where she wanted to be.

She had left behind the sun for a dull dreich morning. August, it was more like November.

The bar was ready to open, Jan Black was efficient as ever, Lynne knew she could rely on her. She was behind the bar tidying and Lynne joined her there.

'My God, you look great,' Jan said jealously.

Lynne had just removed her jacket to reveal she was wearing a green cap sleeved t-shirt, grey leggings and green trainers that showed off her tan to great effect. The look she had been after when she went abroad.

'Thanks,' she smiled. 'Any problems?' Although overseas they had been texting occasionally and no issues were mentioned.

Jan shook her head. 'No. The only thing is Rosie Baker hasn't turned up since Monday.'

'Hasn't turned up? What do you mean, no phone call or anything?

Jan shook her head.

'That's not right, Rosie wouldn't do that.'

Jan never spoke.

'So, she was here on Sunday.'

Jan nodded. 'All day. She was here until we closed at 1 o'clock in the morning.'

'Were there any issues? Any problems with punters, anything like that?'

'No, in fact Sunday was quite quiet after the football.'

'Who was playing?'

'Celtic and Kilmarnock. When Killie got beat most folk left, you know work in the morning that sort of thing.'

Lynne waited before asking- 'did she go home with anybody?'

'I think she went off with her old boyfriend. He was in at one time, they were talking for a while, but you know Rosie.'

Lynne got her phone out. She dialled Rosie's number, but it went straight to answer phone.

The bar door opened, and Emma Boyd walked in. She smiled when she saw Lynne was back. She sat on one of the bar stools and looked her boss over.

'You have had a good holiday,' she gushed.

'You bet. Everything was great, but back to reality. I take it you haven't heard from Rosie Baker. either'

Emma shook her head. 'Not since Sunday afternoon when I left the bar just after 5.'

'She didn't mention anything about George Tate, her ex-boyfriend did she?'

'No. We both know she went with a different guy every night. She was a good time girl, wasn't she?'

Lynne lunged forward as the red mist descended. It was only the bar being between them that stopped her slapping Emma.

Emma jerked back in surprise. Jan grabbed Lynne by the arm, and it seemed to bring her back to her senses.

'I think we need a wee chat in the office Emma dear,' Lynne said when she calmed down. She waited until Emma walked past her as the office was only accessible by going through the bar.

Emma walked slowly as she passed the other 2 women. Lynne had obviously given her a fright. Emma had never seen her like that.

As Lynne went to follow her Jan caught her arm again.

'Stay calm,' she whispered.

'It's ok. I've got it.'

Emma sat down in the dark until the fluorescent light flickered into life. Lynne walked past her and sat behind her computer but didn't switch it on.

It was hard to call it an office, it was a glorified cupboard and felt claustrophobic especially with the tense atmosphere.

Lynne looked at Emma without speaking. The girl was good looking and was an asset to the bar. She was sure some young guys came into the bar just to look at her and chat her up. She would be sorry to lose her when she went back to university in a month or so.

'Sorry about that earlier. I have a soft spot for Rosie, think of her as the daughter I never had. Now, this doesn't go past these 4 walls. Okay.'

Emma nodded but didn't speak.

'Rosie wasn't brought up; she was dragged up. Her stepfather abused her from when she was 13. Her mother was an alcoholic and had only love that was for the bottle. Quite ironic then that Rosie works here in a public bar. Anyway, when she was 16 she ran away and lived in a few hostels. She came to me when she was 18 looking for a job. I didn't need anybody at the time, but you know what her character is, you know easy going and fun loving so I gave her a start and she has been with me ever since. She has her flat now, her only problem is with men.'

She looked at Emma, her expression changed from fear to empathy.

'Rosie never had love growing up and she was looking for it. The only thing she thinks she can give a man for him to love her is sex. It seems crazy to us, but we haven't lived the life she has.'

Emma had tears in her eyes. 'I'm sorry. I didn't know any of this.'

'No, you are the only person I have ever told. Jan knows some of this but doesn't know the full story. Remember when you see Rosie again don't treat her any different, just remember this conversation.'

Back in the bar Lynne put her jacket back on.

'Right, you 2 are in charge, I am going to Rosie's flat to see her, see what's happening. You can manage okay?' she asked with a smile.

'For a wee while, but hurry back,' Jan said laughing.

Lynne stepped out onto the street. Her car was parked behind the bar, but Rosie's flat was only about a mile away. There were other reasons for walking, she would need to drive the long way round the one-way system to get there and parking spaces in that end of town were practically non-existent. Plus, after a week of lazing about she needed the exercise.

Rosie's flat was in Barbadoes Road. The bottom half of Barbadoes Road consisted of 4 in a block red brick flats. Rosie lived in one of the top flats.

Lynne had walked quickly to the area and had worked up a bit of a sweat by the time she got there. The earlier rain left a muggy atmosphere which didn't help her perspiring.

She knew the front door of her flat from the outside; she had dropped Rosie off before. If she remembered correctly Rosie telling her that the top left one was hers.

The front door was closed and locked. There was no buzzer system, so she knocked on the door.

Stepping back there looked like there was no life in any of the flats. She knocked again, this time banging the door with a force a policeman would have been proud of.

Eventually a woman appeared in the opposite upstairs window. She was not happy.

Lynne beckoned her to come down. While she waited she walked back down the path and looked up at Rosie's front window. The curtains were closed, definitely no sign of life.

When Jan said Rosie hadn't turned up deep down Lynne feared for the worst possible outcome. Looking up at her flat window she felt the fear that the worst had happened was becoming a certainty.

The front door of the building opened. Standing there was Shona Murdoch. She was wearing bedclothes, clearly pregnant and not happy at being wakened in the middle of the morning.

Lynne went on the defensive. 'Sorry to get you out of your bed dear. The thing is, I am worried about Rosie Baker. I am her boss at Bar xx. Have you seen her?'

Shona wasn't pacified. 'No.'

'She hasn't been seen or heard of since Monday morning,' Lynne added.

'I was nightshift on Sunday, I haven't seen her since.'

'That doesn't bother you?' Lynne asked.

Shona just shrugged. 'We keep ourselves to ourselves here,' she said. 'Way of the world nowadays.'

'Do you mind if I come in and knock?'

'Knock yourself out,' Shona said then walked away, leaving

Lynne to follow her.

Upstairs Lynne walked over and knocked on Rosie's door. Then she shouted in the letterbox. All the time Shona stood behind her but nearer her own flat door, tired and desperate to get back to bed.

Lynne turned. 'Looks like I will need to get the police.'

Shona shrugged again. 'You do that, but they won't bother if it's only been 2 days she's been missing. Anyway, I am going back to bed.'

Lynne walked back downstairs. At the front door she put the door on the snib, pulling it shut but knowing it wouldn't lock behind her.

Lynne walked back through the park opposite and up to the police station. She could have phoned 101 and spoke to an answerphone, maybe eventually a human, who would tell her they would call round in 2 or 3 days, if, of course, Rosie hadn't turned up again.

She knew enough cops at the station to get a swifter service. Bar XX was their unofficial watering hole; if they wanted service they better give her some help.

At the reception desk at the cop shop a female uniformed officer appeared. She recognised Lynne immediately.

'Hi Lynne. You look good, have you been on holiday?' she asked, noticing the lovely tan.

'Yes, but I have a more important issue. Rosie Baker is missing. I think something has happened to her.'

'What Rosie, your barmaid?'

'Yes. We have had no contact since the early hours of Monday morning. That's not like her. If she wasn't turning out for work she would have at the very least texted me.'

'Yes, but if it's only 2 days we shouldn't deal with it. We would normally wait at least 4 days before sending somebody out.'

'Yes, but this is not normal. Rosie wouldn't not answer my calls anytime. Now her phone is dead.'

The uniform was silent as she thought of her next excuse to get rid of Lynne. Lynne beat her to it.

'Get somebody from C.I.D. down. I want somebody now.'

P.C. Morgan was going to ignore her and try another tactic, but shrewdly opted to pass her on. She dialled the S.C.S. number.

D.S. John Rose had been sitting at his desk for 2 full days and nearly half of the third when the office phone rang.

It's piercing noise echoed through the room with an annoying shrill that no-one else seemed to notice. John took the call.

'Yes, sir, there is a lady in reception wishing to report a missing person.'

Having spent his time since arriving at Kilmarnock trawling through records aimlessly he thought this was a good way out.

'I will be there in a minute,' he answered.

In the reception area he found an attractive woman, possibly mid-fifties waiting for him.

She smiled but didn't recognise him as a pub regular.

'You have a missing person,' he asked her.

'Yes. Well, at least I think so. Rosie Baker, one of my barmaids hasn't been seen since finishing work on Sunday night, well in the early hours of Monday morning.'

'Just not seen?' John asked.

'No. She hasn't been seen or heard of, didn't contact the bar when she was supposed to be working on Monday afternoon which isn't like her and her phone is dead now.'

'No phone, well that's serious,' John said, trying to make a light-hearted joke of it. Lynne didn't appreciate the humour.

'What do you want us to do? Go round there?'

'Yes. I have been down there, there was no sign of life.'

'Right, wait until I get my coat. Looks as if we could get the rain again.'

John hadn't asked for a police car yet so walked round to his own car with Lynne.

When they got in John realised they still hadn't introduced themselves.

'Oh, by the way I am Detective Sergeant John Rose, but you can call me Detective Sergeant.' He hoped that would break the ice, his last attempt at humour failed.

Lynne offered her hand to shake. 'Lynne Murdoch, you can call me anytime.' They both laughed, the ice was smashed.

On the 5-minute journey she told him all her holiday. He could have been bored, listening about food, drink and lazing by the pool, instead he was jealous. It sounded like a great holiday.

Then she told him some of Rosie's checkered history, it didn't make good listening to. As he neared the address he hoped for the best, but he started to fear for the worst.

John parked the car straight outside the building in Barbadoes Road. When he got out he scoped the building. It was mid-terrace so no way through to the back door.

Lynne had already told him it was one of the upstairs flats. She pointed up to it.

'It's the one on the left. We can get in the building, I left the close door open,' Lynne told him.

'That's handy,' he said, watching as the door opened to Lynne's touch.

Outside Rosie's door John took command. He gave the door a good policeman's knock. No response. He knocked it again. The noise would have woken the dead. Instead, it woke Shona next door who stepped out of her flat.

'Oh, you again,' she said from behind them.

'Sorry. He is a police officer,' Lynne said by way of excuse.

'Right, I am going back to bed,' Shona said before quickly going back indoors.

'Do you know if anybody else have a key?,' the D.S. asked Lynne.

'No.'

'Tried under the mat?'

'Rosie wouldn't be that stupid.'

John reached down and lifted the mat up. Nothing, except

a big leggy spider that ran towards Lynne. She screamed then tried to step on it but missed. It scuttled towards the other flat.

Meanwhile John was reaching his hand in the letterbox.

'Oh,' he said, as he felt a length of string inside. Judging by the weight on the end he guessed there was a key attached. His instinct told him if there was to be a crime scene inside then there could be fingerprint on the key, he needed gloves.

'Is there a key? Lynne asked.

'Feels like it, I need to get examination gloves from the car.'

'Why did I not think about checking there,' Lynne said.

'Because most people are more security conscious nowadays.'

'No, Rosie always thought the best in people. Well, after she left home that is, and realised not everyone was evil.'

'Right, I want you to go back outside,' John said.

'But I,' she said, then realised why she had to go out.

John walked down with her. 'Lynne, did you see the nameplate on the door of the woman across the landing from Rosie's? Murdoch. You are Murdoch, aren't you?'

'Yes, but I am sure we aren't related. Must be a coincidence, I am not from here. Originally I am from Glasgow.'

Outside Lynne stood just in the chipped garden area looking up at the windows of Rosie's flat.

John got a handful of blue examination gloves, and a pair of shoe covers from the boot of his car. He left the anxious bar owner and walked back up to the flat.

Sure enough, there was a key on the end of the string when he pulled it out. John opened the door and stepped into the hallway. The first thing that hit him was the heat. Somebody had turned the thermostat up well past normal temperature. It was warmer than the island of Barbados itself in there.

He glanced in the kitchen. Empty and seemed to be no sign of a struggle. Bathroom was empty too. Nothing out of the norm there at first glance either. Living room was empty, only 1 room left to check.

The bedroom door swung open easily straight away John

saw a body on the bed. She was lying straight up in the middle of the bed as if she was sleeping.

'Rosie!' he cried out. He knew it was futile, he was sure from her pallor she was dead.

He walked over to check for signs of life, even from the side of the bed he knew there wouldn't be any.

Knowing it was a crime scene he called it in. That was the easy part, now he had to tell Lynne Murdoch she needed a new barmaid.

Before leaving the flat he delicately turned the thermostat down to minimum. Like the key, there could be prints on the thermostat dial.

Outside on the landing John stopped for a breather. The front door was fully open, and it left a nice cool feeling at the top of the stairs after the oven of indoors.

As he stood there he looked out the landing window to the shared gardens of all the row of flats. In the distance he could see a white-haired old man cutting their square of grass, hurrying before the forecasted rain appeared.

Soon that would be all he would have to worry about, how to get his day in. Retirement in 2 months. What if they hadn't solved this murder by then? Would they ask him to stay on? If they didn't, would they let him if he asked? That was for the future, now he had to face the woman down the stairs waiting for news of what he found.

Pulling the door closed he walked slowly down the stairs.

John didn't have to tell Lynne what he found when he walked outside, his expression did it for him.

'No. No way, she can't be dead.'

'I am afraid there was no sign of life.'

'How, you know, did it happen? Was she,' she started to ask then couldn't say the m word.

'Too early to know,' he lied. 'I have called it in. We will get the scene of crime team first then there will be a postmortem, probably tomorrow. That's when we will know.'

John already knew her cause of death; she had been

strangled. There were marks on her neck, looked like some kind of ligature had been used.

'Is it okay if I sit in your car just now?' she asked.

'Sure. There is the coffee shop at the end of the road, you could grab a drink. It could be a while before SOCO's get here. When they get here I will take you where you want to go.'

'The whatto?'

'SOCO, scene of crime officers.'

'Oh, right. Thanks for your help,' she said. 'I would prefer to just sit in your car.' She was close to tears as she walked away and got into John's Audi.

Within an hour the SOC team arrived, John told them what to expect then handed the lead man the front door key. He told them the heating had been up at maximum in case that was a factor in determining the time of death, although he knew that wouldn't come up until the postmortem.

A few minutes later D.I. Fields arrived with D.C. Sneddon and D.C. Muir.

'What have we got John?'

'Looks like murder, ma'am. Young woman, about 23 years old her boss said, last seen the early hours of Monday morning.'

'Who is that in the car?'

'The woman's boss, she owns the bar the girl worked in.'

'Is it Rosie Baker?' one of the D.C.'s asked. What little colour he had drained from his face as he waited on the answer.

John confirmed it but the young cop already knew.

'There is something I need to tell you,' he said, looking at John and the boss.

Chris moved away from the other D.C. Muir so he couldn't hear their conversation, John and D.C. Colin Sneddon followed her.

'Ma'am, there is something I need to tell you. I was with Rosie Baker on Sunday night after her shift,' Colin said.

The Inspector's stared at him incredulously. She swallowed before saying- 'what do you mean, you walked her home.'

'No, more than that.'

'For fuck's sake man. You slept with her.'

He nodded, as if speaking was too hard a thing to do.

'Why the fuck did you do that?'

'Well, I didn't know she would be murdered, and I would be a witness.'

'A witness. Right now, you are our number 1 suspect.'

'Right, Colin, Alfie Muir will take you back to the station. Wait there until John gets back to interview you. Don't mention a word of this to anyone. Clear?'

'Clear.'

'Not even Alfie Muir.'

'Sure.'

'That means no-one, or you will have me to answer to.'

Colin walked over to the Alfie Muir who was wondering what was going on. Colin just said he had to go back to the station.

'Right, John, question him as a suspect. Don't spare him anything. You better take the woman where she wants to go first.' Chris said.

'Yes, she's been waiting a wee while, but I don't think she is in a great hurry to go back and tell the others about Rosie.

'What you need to know is Rosie's flat is the top left one. Top right is Shona Murdoch who was nightshift and not happy to get wakened up. Don't know who lives in the bottom 2 flats. I will leave that to you.'

'Remember, go hard on that idiot Sneddon.'

INTERVIEW NO.1 WITH
D.C. COLIN SNEDDON

Interview with Detective Constable Colin Sneddon, Present are Colin Sneddon, Detective Sergeant John Rose, Detective Constable Anne Wyper. Wednesday 7th August 11:20.

Anne asked Sneddon if he wanted the services of a lawyer or the police rep both of which he declined.

John: Tell me about Sunday night.

Colin: I was in Bar xx with a couple of my mates. They left about 11 o'clock because they had work in the morning.

I had the Monday off so stayed until shutting time. I was sitting at the bar, and I heard Rosie and some guy having words. After he left I heard her saying to another barmaid she was scared that he might follow her back to her flat.

I gave her the chat; said I was a cop and if she wanted I would walk her back down the road. She never said anything until later. When the bar was closing she asked me if I would walk her back, and I did.

John: Was there any sign of the guy?'

Colin: No. The street was pretty quiet. Anyway, we get back to hers and she invites me in for coffee. We missed out on the coffee and went straight to bed. Had sex, then I left.

John: Last of the great romantics. Describe the guy she was arguing with.

Colin: About 6 foot tall, quite wiry, aged about 30 to 35, reddish hair. Indian ink tattoo on his hand. That was about it.

John: Right, you obviously know you are off the case and will need to be deployed elsewhere. I am sure the Detective Inspector will find you somewhere nice. Interview terminated at 11:35.

BARBADOES ROAD 12:00

JOHN MADE it back to the crime scene just after 12 o'clock. He knew it was going to be a late one and phoned his wife to warn her. For his trouble he got a severe earbashing. Why was he working late when he was retiring? She wasn't cooking all hours of the day for him. Blah, blah, blah. He tried to explain still being an active detective wasn't a job it was a calling, but it hadn't changed anything. He knew he was in for another earbashing when he eventually got home that night, or next morning.

The scene when he parked up was different than the one he had left. There were police cars and vans everywhere. Uniforms were doing door-to-door already and there were 2 cops at the front of the close door.

John put his warrant card in its plastic cover and put it round his neck as he approached them.

'Where is Inspector Field?' he asked.

'She is in the downstairs flat with the tenant. He arrived back 5 minutes ago.'

John walked past them and saw the front door to the flat was open. This was the flat opposite the Murdoch's.

The tenant was sitting down on an armchair while Field and D.C. Alfie Muir stood in the middle of the living room. Muir was taking notes.

'She was leaving for work as you were going to the football. About 1 o'clock on Sunday,' Field said, obviously repeating it to make sure Muir had written it down correctly..

John watched the guy nod. He was in his forties, with a

receding hair line, what hair he had was lank black shoulder length hair that looked as if it hadn't seen shampoo for days and stubble that wasn't designer. He looked nervous, there again if he had never been interviewed by the police what else could be expected.

'Did you speak to her?'

'Aye. She asked who we were playing, and did I think we would win. I told her we beat Celtic last year; we weren't scared of them. When we got to the end of the road she crossed over and said good luck. That was the last thing she said to me.'

Tears formed in his eyes, and he wiped them with the sleeve of his overalls. 'Sorry,' he said,

'We know it's been a shock to everyone. Did you hear her come back in after her work on Sunday night, well Monday morning?'

'No. I had a couple of beers because we got thumped and slept soundly. First thing I heard was when I got up for a pee, the beer does that to me and as I was going back to bed the front door slammed shut. I went to the living room window and saw her ex-boyfriend walking past.'

The Inspector looked out the window. 'Which way was he going?'

The tenant pointed to the right which was away from the beginning of the street.

While Field was asking the questions John looked round the room trying to work out something about the guy. The décor was bland. The feature wall was plain light blue, the rest plain white, obviously a tribute to his local football team. There was a Kilmarnock team calendar on the wall but nothing else. Apart from the large sofa and chairs, also in light blue leather and the big telly on its unit there was nothing else. Except, strangely, a row of large jar Yankee candles on a shelf at the bay window. Nothing else, no vase, no photographs. Definitely a bachelor's room.

'Do you live alone, Mister McQueen?'

'Yes.'

John took a few steps back then looked in the bedroom. The bed was unmade and there were clothes scattered on the floor. There was a whiff of stale sweat and another unmistakeable smell in the room. Faint, but definitely there.

The kitchen was similar, a load of dishes at the sink waiting to be washed. John smiled, his flat would be like that without Karen to make sure he kept it clean and tidy.

John walked back into the living room as the D.I. was finishing.

'Right, Mister McQueen, here's my card. If you remember anything give me a ring.'

He leaned up and took the card, looking at it carefully.

John stepped forward.

'Hi. What's your first name?'

He looked surprised, thought the interview was over. 'It's Joe.'

'Joe, I am not asking you this to get you into trouble, so be honest. Do you smoke cannabis?'

'No,' he said, fear suddenly in his eyes.

'Why do you have all the candles?'

'I like candles. Candles smell nice.'

John suddenly thought Joe might not have a very high I.Q., he hadn't noticed it before when he was answering questions.

'Look, be honest, you aren't in any trouble for it, but I can smell it in your bedroom.'

'It's the folk round about. I can hardly open my windows because the smell comes in. I hate the smell of it.'

'Which neighbours is it?'

Joe shrugged. 'Don't know.'

'Did Rosie smoke drugs?'

Joe's expression changed from fear to anger. 'Only when he was with him?'

'Who, Joe?'

'The ex-boyfriend. They would sit outside puffing away and laughing and giggling.'

'You liked her Joe.'

He nodded. 'She was nice. He wasn't.'

John turned to the other 2 detectives. 'That's all I wanted to know.'

'Right,' Field said, 'remember, if there is anything else you can think of give me a call.'

They walked into the outside hallway and closed the door behind them.

'Anything from the SOC team?' John asked.

'Off the record, definitely murder and it's been a couple of days,' Field said.

'Have you interviewed the upstairs woman?'

'Shona, yes, we got a statement earlier. I told her about Rosie's demise. She didn't seem bothered to tell you the truth. All she said was the usual "kept themselves to themselves" story. Got the feeling she wasn't Rosie's biggest fan. Her husband has 2 or 3 part-time jobs, expects him back around 3 o'clock,' Field said.

'What about the other downstairs neighbour?'

'Shona said she didn't really know her, bit of a recluse, rarely went out. She said her husband did some odd jobs for her about the flat and told her she was going to stay with relatives and hadn't been seen since around Easter.'

'That just leaves her and the husband to interview then we will be finished for today,' John said.

'Yes, once the reports are written up we can head home,' his boss said with a smile.

Inwardly John groaned, he hated paperwork.

As they stood talking at the bottom of the stone staircase there was a noise at front door.

They looked round and saw a man who wanted to get in. The P.C. waved and D.I. Field walked down to see who it was. She returned accompanied by the man who was very agitated.

'Just got the message, I was out this couple's back door. Can't believe she is dead,' he said.

As they reached the others the Inspector introduced Andy Murdoch, Shona's husband, to the other 2 cops.

Slowly they walked up the stairs. Andy paused at the top landing and looked into Rosie's flat as the front door was opened. The white suited SOC team could clearly be seen gathering evidence.

'Oh, I don't think there is any point checking the staircase, I brushed and mopped it on Monday,' Andy said.

'That's lucky, if you hadn't you would all have been put in temporary accommodation,' John said.

'It's normally every Tuesday it was done but there was mud splattered inside the front door,' Andy explained. 'Didn't want it trekked in to the house.'

The front door to the Murdoch flat swung open as they reached it. Obviously Shona had been watching for her husband's arrival.

They followed her into the living room.

'Can I get changed first,' Andy asked. He was wearing jeans and a jacket that were covered in paint and other signs of work.

'Of course. You wouldn't get sitting on my sofa with those clothes on,' Fields said. It might have sounded like a joke if it wasn't for her deadpan delivery.

D.I. Fields and D.C. Alfie Muir sat on the sofa, Shona sat on one of the 2 chairs while D.S. John Rose walked over towards the window, looking out as he did.

Shona Murdoch had already given a statement. John didn't know what was in it so didn't know if there was anything else to ask her. It seemed nobody else did so they sat in a strange silence.

John was annoyed by the atmosphere and broke the quiet.

'You work nightshifts, Shona. What do you work at?'

'I am a nurse in the A and E at the hospital.'

'Are you working tonight?' he asked.

'No,' she answered. 'Sunday was my last scheduled shift, last night was overtime.'

'How are things at, I take it you work at Crosshouse hospital.'

'Yes. It's crazy most nights, especially at the weekends. People think Covid has gone but the wards are full of it. Add to that the drunks at the weekends, you will know about them.'

John nodded, but it was years since he had been there. Is it 12 hour shifts you do?'

'Yes, but by the time we do our handovers it can be more like 12 and a ½.'

'Must be a struggle, you know with the pregnancy.'

She never got to answer as Andy appeared in the room.

'Take a seat, sir,' Field said.

Andy sat in the empty chair. John could see his hand was shaking a bit.

'This is just an informal interview,' she started. 'So, when did you last see Rosie?'

Andy thought. 'Sunday probably. I was just coming back from a job as she was going out to work. Must have been about 1 o'clock.'

'Seem happy enough?'

'Yes.

'On her own?'

He nodded. 'Joe McQueen was walking behind her as I drove past. I waved to her, and she waved back. I waved at him too, but he didn't see me.'

'Did you speak to her much? Not on Sunday, but in general.'

'Just in the passing. That you off to work, are you working tonight, you know. Just chit-chat. I knew she was a barmaid.'

'Were you ever in her flat?'

'How do you mean?'

'Inside it. Especially in the last few weeks, say.'

'Why?'

'Well, they are gathering forensics as you saw. If you have been in there will be traces.'

'No. Shona love, could you make me a coffee? I've not had a drink since 10 o'clock this morning.'

'Okay. Do any of you want coffee or tea?'

The police officers all declined, and Shona left the room. As soon as she was out of earshot Andy leaned in towards the Detective Inspector.

'Sorry, but I was in there, what about 2 or 3 weeks ago. Her power was tripping, and I showed her how to reset the fuse board. I never told Shona, she gets very jealous, and she says Rosie is a tart.'

'Okay, well we will almost certainly need a DNA sample from you to rule you out. Why would your wife say Rosie was a tart?'

'Well, it wasn't a different man every night if that's what she said. Although since she split up with that junkie guy there have been a few men in visiting, if you know what I mean. Shona would say Tom last night Dick tonight, Harry tomorrow night no doubt.'

'Funny Shona didn't mention any of that to us,' the Inspector said in response. 'Maybe not wanting to speak ill of the dead.'

Shona walked in carrying her husband's mug of coffee.

'What about the woman downstairs?' John asked.

Andy looked round. He had almost forgotten the Detective Sergeant was there.

'Oh, old Mrs. Muldoon. She has not been around since Easter. Told me she was going to stay with an old friend in Glasgow, haven't seen her since.

'You know her quite well?' John continued.

'I did some wee odd jobs for her. Took her bins out and that kind of thing.'

'What is it you do yourself?' he asked. Field might have asked his wife the question earlier, but she liked to hear things from the horse's mouth.

'I do match day stewarding at Rugby Park. I also do general DIY, grass cutting, trimming bushes, painting, all that kind of thing.'

'Did you do anything for Mrs. Muldoon?'

'Just wee bits and pieces. At her age she didn't like getting disturbed. She was rarely out of the house.'

'Yet she went to all the way to Glasgow to live with a relative.'

'A friend, she said,' Andy corrected John.

John smiled. When people rehearsed what they were going to say they liked it to be perfect. John thought Andy was talking himself into being more of a suspect every time he spoke.

'You don't have a key for her house?' John said as a follow up.

'No.'

'You had a key at one time,' Shona said. 'Remember when you were doing that bit of tiling for her earlier in the year.'

For once her husband looked short of an answer. Trying to think what his wife was talking about.

'Oh, yes. That's right. I gave her it back. You know what old people are like, I was scared she would accuse me of stealing or something. She accused Joe down stairs of looking in her bedroom window at night.'

'You don't think he did, then?'

'Why would he, the woman was 74?'

John looked at his boss, signalling he was finished with his questioning for now.

'Okay, Andy, Shona, we will get out of your hair. Leave you to drink your coffee in peace,' D.I. Field said then got up to leave. 'Your wife has my card if there is anything that you remember or want to tell us just give us a call.'

Andy took his first sip of coffee while his wife showed the cops out.

When they walked out they saw the front door to Rosie's flat was still open. They walked down the stairs and out in reverential silence.

Outside they could see the uniforms were near the end of the street in both sides and directions.

'Right, let's get back to the station, get everything written up and see where we go from here,' the Detective Inspector said.

INCIDENT ROOM, 17:00

THE ROOM was full, all the Detectives involved, the other detectives left in the department and the 8 uniformed officers who had carried out door-to-door were present.

D.I. Field stood at the whiteboard, Operation Barbadoes Girl was the title at the top. Rosie Baker's name was at the top.

To the left were the names Colin Sneddon, George Tate, Andy Murdoch and Joe McQueen.

As John looked at the board he wondered why she hadn't written D.C. before Sneddon's name. If word wasn't already out about his involvement it soon would be.

'Okay, first thing we need to do is talk to George Tate. He would appear to be our number 1 suspect.' He looked round for a volunteer. D.C. Alfie Muir put his hand up.

'I know him, sir. Brought him in several times,' Muir said.

'Anything significant from the door-to-door folks?'

He looked round all 8 officers. One put a hand up.

'A few of the neighbours knew her to look at but that was about it.'

Another 1 or 2 P.C.'s agreed but said nothing more.

'Okay, you can go. Thanks for today.'

The plods walked out leaving only the detectives in the room. Alfie Muir was on his computer, checking on George Tate and his police record. There were a number of addresses for him.

'Okay next steps for tomorrow. Firstly, I would like a word with Mister Tate before the postmortem which will no doubt be tomorrow. John, what are you up to?'

'I have arranged to interview Lynne Murdoch at 9 o'clock tomorrow morning. She is going to arrange for the other full-time barmaids to be there between 9 and 10.'

'Good thinking. I reckon the post mortem won't happen before 11 o'clock. You and I should attend it John.'

John nodded. As much as he hated going to postmortems it was his duty.

There was something buzzing about his head, and he needed to get it out. 'Something that bothers me ma'am. Iris Muldoon. A recluse that hasn't been seen since Easter time. Over 4 months and her neighbours haven't batted an eyelid.'

'Yes, I wondered about that too. Natasha!' she called.

A young Detective Constable looked over.

'Iris Muldoon, the neighbour. See what you can find out about her. Supposedly visiting a friend in Glasgow.'

'Is that all we have?' she asked.

It wasn't what she said that narked the Inspector, but the way she said it.

'Yes. You are a detective, well detect.'

'Okay, Detective Constable Garret, are you working on anything desperately urgent at the moment?'

Garret tried to think of something quickly, the boss beat him to it.

'No? Good. Tomorrow first thing I want you to start at Barbadoes Road and make your way to Bar XX checking for CCTV or Ring doorbells. Rosie Baker walked home from the pub so she must have been caught on camera at some point. Okay.'

Reluctantly the young D.C nodded agreement. He knew it was a crap task, especially if the weather didn't improve.

'Right, that's us for today. Except you Alfie. I want you to find Tate and arrange for him to be here first thing tomorrow.

8TH AUGUST 2024 BAR XX 09:00

JOHN PARKED his car in the police car park and walked up the John Finnie Street to Bar XX. Inside the bar was lit up, but the front door was closed when he tried to open it.

Knocking on the window the door quickly opened. Lynne Murdoch popped her head round the door and waved him in.

When he walked past she closed the door and locked it behind him. Then she showed him over to a table in the corner of the pub, as far from the bar as they could be.

There was a coffee sitting at one side of the table, he guessed this was where Lynne wanted to sit, so sat opposite.

'Do you want a coffee or tea? I can't offer you anything stronger.'

'No, I am okay just now.'

Lynne was wearing black today, understandably.

'I thought about closing the bar for a few days, but Rosie wouldn't have wanted it. Truth be told, I couldn't afford it either.'

'Not any easier this morning, is it?'

'No.'

'You know, for all I never met her I feel I know her. You told me so much yesterday I get that feeling. More than ever, I want to get the bastard that did this.'

'So, it is murder,' Lynne said.

John had slipped up by saying too much. 'Surely you knew,' he said, trying to cover his error.

Lynne nodded. 'Not 100%, but I was pretty sure.'

'Now though, I want more details. Anything that can help nail the murderer. It might be tough at times, but that's the way it has to be. I am sure you understand.'

'Of course. Where should I start?'

'You don't mind if I record this,' he asked, knowing there would be too much info for him to remember and write down later.

She nodded and John pulled out an old-fashioned personal recorder, the kind that used small tapes.

'Start with her relationship with her ex-boyfriend.'

'George Tate. She was besotted with him and went with him for about 6 months. About 2 months ago he cheated on her, and she kicked him to the kerb. I heard he was back in the bar on Sunday night. Must have heard I was on holiday because I would have told him to sling his hook if I was here.'

'Was the relationship good, you know did he treat her well?'

'No. He never had any money. He would turn up here sponging drink or money off her. The worst thing was he got her smoking weed. It didn't affect her work or anything. She always smelled nice sometimes there was a whiff of it.'

'What happened after they split up?'

Lynne shook her head. 'She went off the rails a bit. With men I mean. She would lie in bed with anybody she could. Maybe not just anybody, but she had more than her share.'

'Who, customers?'

Lynne nodded. 'As far as I knew a few of them. She did say something about a neighbour, but I didn't get his name. Then she let slip she went to bed with one of the taxi drivers. I pay for all my staff to get home safely, use the same company, so I can get you his name.'

'Great. Anything else you know that might help?'

Lynne shook her head.

'Well, you have my card.' John looked up and saw there was a woman working behind the bar. 'Will she be next?' John asked, motioning to the woman.

'Yes, that's my manager Jan Todd.'

'Jan, you are up next!' Lynne called over to her.

Jan dried her hands on a towel and walked round from the bar. Lynne left and spoke as they met, Jan telling her boss what she had been doing.

Jan walked over and sat across from John. She looked nervous.

'Jan, is it?'

She nodded.

'This is nothing to worry about. You won't be going to court or anything, I just want to get as much background about Rosie as I can.'

Jan swallowed hard at the mention of the murdered girl's name.

'I heard George Tate was in on Sunday night. Rosie was talking to him. Correct?'

'Yes. He was giving her all the chat about how he was sorry, and it was the biggest regret in his life that they split up. It's not as if he was whispering, he is the kind of guy that likes to be heard. You know even when he whispers everybody within earshot hears.

I think she was going to go for it until one of her friends came in and told her he tried to get off with her in another pub earlier.

He had nipped to the toilet at the time, when he came back and saw her friend was at the bar he knew he had blown it, but still tried to talk his way around her.'

'Did he leave after that?'

'Yes, she had bought him a drink but took it from the bar

and poured it down the sink. He stormed out but turned at the front door and pointed at her.'

'What in a threatening manner?'

'Yes. He never said anything, but she was scared after he left.'

'Did she go home in the taxi?'

'No. She said she was going to a party with a guy.'

'Do you know him?'

'I don't know his name, but I would recognise him if I saw him again. He said he was a cop, but that might just have been chat.'

John was relieved, at least for the moment. Last thing they needed then was media speculation about Sneddon's part in the investigation.

'Anything else you know might help us in the investigation?'

She shook her head.

'Okay, here is my card. Anything comes to mind, even something you might think is trivial then call me.'

Jan left and Lynne walked over.

'Still don't want a coffee. My other 2 regular barmaids should have been here by now. You can have a drink while you are waiting.'

'Okay, coffee it is. 2 sugar and milk.'

'Jan, 2 coffees, just the way I like them.'

She sat down opposite John. She seemed a bubbly type of character, but she suddenly looked serious.

'You saw Rosie, how was she murdered?' she asked.

It hung in the air. She obviously knew the previous day he had bullshitted her with the waffle about having to wait until after postmortem although she didn't mention it then. Now he had admitted how she was killed she wanted more detail.

'Between you and me,' he said then stopped as he saw Jan approaching. He waited until she had left their drinks on the table and left before continuing.

John had his hand on the table. Lynne reached over and

gently touched his fingers with hers.

'Just between us,' she said. John felt a spark and wondered whether she was coming on to him or was she just using her feminine charm to find out what she wanted.

'She was strangled.'

He wasn't surprised by her reaction, she cried. It was probably the first release of grief she had since she found out Rosie was dead.

There was another knock on the window. Jan went to the door and let the 2 barmaids in. John looked over and thought at first it was 2 schoolgirls. Maybe they weren't that young on second look, he was just getting old.

Lynne regained her composure, dried her tears, then got up and lifted her coffee. 'I will leave you to interview these 2,' she said as she left.

As she walked away she turned and spoke to him. 'Thanks for that, you didn't need to tell me,' she said, them left him.

John spoke to the 2 girls individually as he drank his coffee. He got more out of his coffee really. As they spoke they constantly used "you know" and "she was like". Were young folk all airheads now, he wondered.

When the second girl left the table Lynne walked back over.

'Got all you need?' she asked, back smiling now.

'Enough to be getting on with.'

'It's been nice meeting you, shame it wasn't under different circumstances.'

John got up and moved close to her.

'Now I know you are here I might pop in. The coffee was really good.'

'There's more to entertain you in here than coffee,' she said in a whisper.

'Anyway, I must go. My boss has already messaged me.'

Lynne showed him out.

John walked back to the police station. All the time thinking more about Lynne Murdoch than Rosie Barker.

8TH AUGUST 2024 11:00 THE MORGUE, CROSSHOUSE HOSPITAL

JOHN AND Chris Fields sat together in the viewing gallery at the morgue. Chris had a medical mask on. She offered one to John, but he refused. It didn't stop the smell unless you put Vic or another strong smell blocker in it.

The pathologist appeared and introduced himself. He spoke all through the postmortem but had a speech impediment and John struggled to understand him. Chris continually nodded her head as if she was following his commentary. An hour and a half later they were seated in the D.I.'s police car, John was in the driving seat.

'I don't know how you could follow what he was saying,' John said.

'I didn't understand very much at all, but he kept looking straight at me, I was just nodding to be polite.'

John laughed. He was surprised at the spiky woman next to him could be nice to somebody.

'All I got was she was strangled by a smooth cord or similar, from behind, sometime on Monday morning. There was also the mention of the thermostat being set too high to make the time of death hard to estimate.'

'Yes. Not much for an hour and a half which is an hour and a half of my life I will never get back, a numb arse and a smell that will take days to clear from my senses for a result we could have guessed. This job can be shit at times.'

'I agree. Did you interview Tate this morning?'

'No. Uniform couldn't locate him. They had since 6 o'clock last night.'

The D.I.'s phone buzzed. 'Speak of the devil, they finally caught him. Put your foot down John, I can't wait to put the boot into this streak of pish.'

John picked his way through the hospital car park, once clear he put the foot down.

INTERVIEW NO. 2
GEORGE TATE

Interview with George Tate, present Tate, Detective Sergeant John Rose, Detective Inspector Chris Field, Detective Constable Myra Painter. 08August 13:15

Myra asked Tate if he wanted the duty solicitor or his own brief, he refused both.

Field: Tell me what you were doing on Saturday night.

Tate: I was out on the pull. Round the local pubs, you know.

Field: No, George, we don't know.

Tate: You know, have a few drinks, then pick up a bird, back to hers. Bang bang, you know. What is this all about anyway? Is it illegal to go out on a Saturday night now.

Field: George, you should know we ask the questions.

You were seen Bar XX. Who did you talk to there?

Tate: I was shagging a wee barmaid a few months ago, I wasn't having luck elsewhere, so I gave her the patter, you know, big mistake cheating on her. I went for a slash, when I got back her mate was talking to her. Must have told her I tried to get off with her and she dumped my drink.

Field: When you left you threatened her.

Tate: Is that what she is saying.

Field: She is not saying anything, she is dead. Murdered. We have a witness who puts you in the area at the time we think she was killed.

Tate: Where, at her place? No way man. No, no way. I haven't been there since she dumped me months ago. Not near the place.

Field: How did you know she was killed at her flat, I just said you were seen in the area where she was murdered.

Tate: Well, I just guessed. Look, last I seen her was in the bar.

Field: Where were you then?

Tate: I don't want to say.

Field: George, this isn't you caught with a bit of weed, this is a murder investigation.

Tate: All right. I ended back at my mate's place. He wasn't in and I ended up in bed with his girl.

Field: I need a name, George.

Tate: No way man. He will kill me.

Field: George, George, George, you don't seem to realise how much of the brown stuff you are in. Up to your neck it would seem. You threaten an ex-girlfriend, next morning she turns up dead.

Tate: That's nothing to what Da, nearly said it there. Anyway, I would be wearing a wooden overcoat if he knew what I had done with his bird.

Field: Okay, you can go just now, but remember the drill, no travelling abroad and if you are leaving the district give us a forwarding address.

Interview terminated at 13:30

Tate looked around the other occupants, surprised he

was free to go as easily as he was. He couldn't get out fast enough.

'What's your opinion, John?' Field asked.

'Seems to be telling the truth. He really did seem scared of his so-called mate who he did the dirty on.'

'Thought that myself. We will need to see what we get from forensics. That's about lunchtime. What do you do?'

'The wife makes me sandwiches. Doesn't want me eating too much rubbish.'

'Most days I go to Greggs. Unless it's raining and I send somebody else to get for me. It's good at times being the boss.'

INCIDENT ROOM 13:45

EVERYBODY RE-CONVENED in the incident room for the latest update. D.I. Fields had updated the whiteboard. Somebody had managed to get a picture of Rosie Baker and put it at the top of the board. It made it seem more personal to them in their hunt for the murderer.

'Right folks, what do we have. Rosie Baker reported not been seen since getting back to her flat early hours of Monday morning. Early blood and tissue tests results from the postmortem was that she had small amount of alcohol, but it also revealed she had smoked cannabis very shortly before her death. We will need to follow up a few things with our colleague Colin Sneddon.

John, you spoke with Rosie's work colleagues this morning.'

She turned to John Rose, and he got up to his feet. 'Yes, what they told me was her ex-boyfriend turned up on Sunday night. Tried to get off with her but failed. They, and Rosie, thought he threatened her. We have since interviewed him but released without charge. I also found out she was what my old mother would have called a good-time girl. Different fellow every night, or at least quite a few.'

He turned and looked at the boss as he sat down, indicating he was finished.

'Thanks, John. Detective Constable George Garret, you went looking for CCTV or Ring doorbells. How did you do?'

The D.C. stood up, putting a disappointed look on his face. 'Not good news. I drove from Barbadoes Place all the way back up to Bar XX. Sorry, no success.'

Although John was angry at the detective's sloppiness, John watched D.I. Field's reaction. Her look went from surprise to anger. Anger to rage.

The red colour on her cheeks got brighter by the second until she erupted.

'You drove! You drove the couple of miles! Is this your first major investigation Detective Constable Garret?'

She started loudly but increased volume until her voice seemed to echo around the room.

'No,' he said then added, 'ma'am.'

'Did you not see the sign on the door! You walk past it every day! Serious crime squad with the emphasis on the bloody serious!'

She paused to get her breath back before continuing her tirade. 'It would appear you aren't taking either this investigation or your job very seriously!'

Garret held his head down in shame. The silence in the room was palpable. Although many agreed the boss was correct, the method of her dressing-down was all wrong.

'Are you still here!' she shouted.

Garrett stood up and started walking toward the door but stopped when Field started talking again.

'What you need to do now, Garrett, if it's within your capabilities, is walk from here to Bar XX then walk all the way to Barbadoes Place, noting all the CCTV and Ring doorbells there are and speak to the owners of the premises, explaining to them this is a mur-der enquiry and any images they have are important.'

Garrett made the mistake of looking round as he stood halfway between where he had been sitting and the exit door.

'Nod once if you understand and twice if you want to resign from the force,' Field continued.

Garrett nodded once then scuttled out of the room, leaving the strangest atmosphere behind him.

John, with 20-odd years' experience behind him, hadn't seen a dressing down anything like what he had just witnessed. Although he agreed with the boss' sentiment he disagreed with her methods. Personally, he would take them aside and rip them a new arsehole and only on rare occasions did he find it necessary to do it in front of fellow colleagues.

Field shook her head as Garrett left the room before continuing. 'P.C. Simpson, where are we with Iris Muldoon?'

Natasha stood up, wary of her boss' recent outburst and aware she could be next. 'Boss, I tried all the banks, nobody appeared to have her banking there. Or at least were not willing to talk to police over the phone.'

Field, standing in front of all shook her head.

'However, I phoned all the health centre's she could have used, posing as a concerned niece and although the person at her local centre shouldn't have told me, she said Iris hadn't requested any of her blood pressure tablets since March. The tablets were clearly a prescription item, and she was on the verge of asking for the police to be called in.'

'So where are we?' Field asked, a trace of bitterness still in her voice.

'Ma'am, I would recommend we go in and check her flat out. Even if she was getting her prescription somewhere else it would be on her record as they are all computerised now.'

A smile broke across Chris Field's face. 'Well done. Arrange a uniform to accompany us, we will meet him outside the Muldoon flat at 14 hundred hours.'

Natasha nodded and she also left the room, although in a lot better terms than the previous detective had. She was going to arrange for the uniform officer Field had requested.

'Anybody with anything else to add?' Field said, before ending the meeting.

Field headed back to her office and nodded for John to follow her.

'Looks like your theory about Muldoon is correct,' she said after she sat down behind her desk. 'Unless her health has suddenly improved with a change of air.'

'She was supposed to be staying with a friend in Glasgow. Hardly renowned for its health-giving properties.'

'Quite. Right, let's get moving. Iris Muldoon might be waiting on us. You can drive,' she said, as if he had a choice.

John didn't have to drive; Natasha Simpson was given the keys. John offered to sit in the back but was given the front passenger seat.

BARBADOES ROAD, KILMARNOCK 14:00

JOHN WALKED up to the front door of the block and gave a good old policeman's knock. Upstairs was still an active crime scene, in case forensics wanted to double-check on anything and if none of the other occupants weren't in then the uniform on the door would come down and answer it.

Sure enough, a young bored looking P.C. opened the door a few minutes later.

'The woman in the upstairs flat said you were here,' he said.

'Yes, we are going in to the bottom flat on the left, below the one you are guarding.'

Just as they went to walk in a police van drew up. The P.C. got out, carrying a breaching tool, a large metal bar used to force doors open.

'You will hardly need that,' John joked.

They followed the P.C. in and stood back as he leaned back then with one jab the door flew open. John had been correct.

Having more experience of those type of situations John led the way in. Firstly, he noticed the smell, and the fact there wasn't one. A hint of old woman's must and a background of damp, but nothing more sinister.

Secondly there was a pile of letters behind the door. He reached down and handed them to the D.I. who was following him.

He headed straight for the bedroom. It was neat and tidy; the bed was made and neatly tucked in. Nothing under the bed and no sign of any blood or other sign of a struggle.

Satisfied, he walked into the hallway. Field was in the living room, going through the mail, Simpson in the kitchen.

'Check the fridge,' John called through to her from the hallway.

D.C. Simpson looked puzzled. 'Sir?' she asked as she walked out towards him.

'What do you do if you go on holiday, say for a fortnight?'

This didn't help, she looked even more puzzled.

'You make sure there is nothing in the fridge that could go off while you are away.'

Natasha went a bit red. 'Oh, I still live with my parents, sir. Mum does all that,' she replied. However, she followed orders and opened the upper door, the fridge of the fridge freezer.

'God, that stinks,' she said, closing it again quickly to allow herself to recover.

John left her to it. He had a cursory look in the bathroom, nothing there, then walked to the big cupboard at the end of the hallway. He walked back to the kitchen to see what his junior had found out.

Her redness had faded quickly leaving her a nice shade of puce. 'Sir, most of the stuff has use by dates in April.'

John nodded; it was as he expected. 'Did you check the freezer?'

Natasha looked at him as if he was going to provide another pearl of wisdom and explain the reason for saying that. He didn't, instead, he just stood waiting on her opening the freezer door at the bottom, to see her reaction.

John watched her open the freezer door. She was silent as she looked in. Puzzled, she leaned in closer. Next she started to put her blue gloved in to touch what was there.

'Don't touch!' John shouted.

Natasha jumped back, startled, and looked at John. 'What is it?' she asked.

'It's not what, its who.'

Natasha's mouth opened widely in surprise. 'Misses Muldoon.'

John nodded.

'Oh my God.' She looked in again. 'Poor thing.'

John leaned past her and looked. Somehow the old lady had been forced into an upright position in the otherwise empty freezer.

Over his shoulder Natasha asked a simple question. 'How did you know?'

'Well, the trays and shelves from the freezer are in the hall cupboard so something had to be in there. Call it in, we need forensics here.'

John left her on the phone calling it in and walked through to tell the boss.

'She is in the freezer,' he said.

Field looked up from the sofa she was sitting on. She wasn't surprised. Next to her was a pile of opened mail, more on her lap.

'Somebody has been using her bank card. Drawing 250 pound a week.'

John whistled. 'Did she have a few bob then?'

'She did have in April, but it's been draining away.'

'What do you think we have then? The same killer?'

'Two bodies in the same building? I am not a great believer in coincidence. Especially with dead bodies.'

'What do we do now?' John asked, but he knew the answer.

'We bring Murdoch and McQueen in for questioning.' John nodded in agreement. 'Yes. With the main entrance door being kept locked then surely if somebody else was hanging about the neighbours here would know about it.'

'True. With the woman being pregnant we will just interview her here.'

'Better call for more troops,' John said, going through to find Natasha again.

John Rose knocked on the Murdoch's front door. He was accompanied by Chris Field and 2 uniforms.

'Oh!' Shona said as she opened the door and saw the posse of cops. 'Has there been a development?'

'In a way, yes. Mind if we come in?'

'What, all of you?'

'Depends. Is your husband in?'

She nodded.

'Yes, well we will all be coming in then.'

Andy Murdoch was sitting on the sofa watching a film on the television. He too looked surprised and hit the volume button on the remote to kill the sound.

'What's going on?' he asked.

His wife, who had walked in first just shrugged.

'Earlier today we found the deceased body of your neighbour Iris Muldoon in her home. We would like you to accompany my colleagues to the station to answer some questions.'

Andy looked at his wife then at the Detective Sergeant.

'What, both of us?'

'No sir, just yourself. We will speak to your wife here. Don't worry, it's just a matter of routine, you know with a body found on the premises, especially as it is a second one in a matter of days.'

'Oh right, but I know nothing about it. As far as I knew she was staying in Glasgow.'

'As I said, routine sir. We just need a bit of background.'

Andy got up from the sofa. 'Shouldn't be long, he said to his wife. 'Can I get me coat and stuff?'

'Of course, sir.'

John waited until Andy and the 2 uniforms left the flat before taking a seat on the sofa. Chris sat on the other armchair and took her notebook out. They hadn't discussed it, but John was taking the lead on the interview.

'I don't know if I can help you either,' Shona said.

'You just need to tell us what you know,' the Detective Inspector said reassuringly.

INTERVIEW NO.3
SHONA MURDOCH
AUGUST 08 15:15

Rose: When did you last see Iris Muldoon?

Shona: To tell you the truth I am not too sure. Must have been round about Easter. Yes, probably the week before, she gave me an Easter card. Did it every year.

Rose: How long have you stayed here, in the flat?

Shona: Two, no three years. It was just as lockdown was coming to an end and things were moving again.

Rose: How long have Andy and you been married?'

Shona: What? What has that got to do with Mrs. Muldoon's death.

Rose: As we said earlier, it's just background.

Shona: Five years if you must know. For the record we lived in rented accommodation in Hurlford before buying here. I can give you the old address if you want.

Rose: That won't be necessary. Your husband said he is a part-time sort of odd job man; does he earn a lot?

Shona: Enough. I am the main bread winner. He

resents it at times, but he hasn't been able to hold down a full-time job for years.

Rose: Oh, why's that?

Shona: He doesn't like being told what to do. That's why being his own boss suits him.

Rose: When you say he doesn't like being told what to do. Does he get angry when ordered about, does he have a short temper?'

Shona: No. Nothing like that.

Rose: Then why can't he keep a full-time job?

Shona: He can be a bit cheeky. Well ratty at times, but he is not a violent man.

Rose: Did he ever do any jobs for Iris?'

Shona: Yes, occasionally. She was very strong willed, didn't like asking people for help, but if something beat her she would ask Andy to help her or if he knew anybody who could do what she needed.

Field: Andy was her go-to-guy then. I live alone and sometimes I wish I had a man about the house.

Shona: Yes, I guess you could say that.

Rose: When was the last time he did anything for her?

Shona: Oh, I think it was the week before Easter. Yes, when she gave me the Easter card she wondered if Andy could fix her bedroom light for her.

Rose: So, he fixed it for her.

Shona: Yes, that was when she told him she was going to a friends to stay for Easter.

Rose: Strange she didn't tell you. I mean, by all accounts she was never out of the house. I

	would have thought she would have told you when she gave you the Easter card.
Shona:	As I said, we all keep ourselves to ourselves here.
	In fact, he said she never paid him for the job. He had to go and get a new bulb holder. She was upset at the time because she didn't have any cash in her purse that day. He went down on the Tuesday after Easter and said she wasn't in. It was only a couple of pounds, so he wasn't that bothered.
Rose:	Right, well I think we have enough background. We will speak to Andy now and get him back to you as soon as we can. Have you anything more to ask, ma'am?
Field:	No. You have our card, Shona, if anything comes up, don't hesitate to get in touch. Oh, one thing, you or Andy don't have a key to Missus Muldoon's flat, do you.
Shona:	No.
Field:	Have you ever had a key?
Shona:	There was one time, just after we moved in. She went to her friends in Glasgow then and we kept an eye on the place. Well, Andy did mostly. I was dayshift at the time, so he was about more during the day.
Field:	You gave her it back then?
Shona:	Yes. She asked for it. Andy said he was quite insistent about it.
Field:	Fine. That's it then, we will be getting out of your hair.
Shona:	How long will Andy be?'
Field:	I am sure he will be back this evening.

John drove them back to the police station; Natasha had already been given a lift.

'Well, what's your feel for things, John?' the boss asked.

'Murdoch might be the man, if he is Shona knows nothing about it,' he answered. 'Seems funny he was the only person Iris spoke to.'

'Yes I think you are right. Let's nip round to Tesco's first.'

'Need some shopping?'

'Ha ha. We are on duty John. Can't rip the staff a new arsehole then be unprofessional ourselves.

No, most of the cash withdrawals have been made at the cash machine there. If there is CCTV we will have the person bang to rights.'

John was parked up within 5 minutes, the supermarket was only 2 streets away from Barbadoes Road. They walked past the entrance to the cash machine area.

'Bingo,' Chris said as she pointed up at the camera trained on the machines. 'Let's just hope the bloody thing is working.'

The security guard at the podium inside the shop smiled at Chris when she approached him. His smile didn't change when she showed him her warrant card.

'How can I help?'

'Tell me something, is the camera at the cash machine working?'

'Yes. It's working. All the cameras are.'

'Can you give us a copy of say the last 3 months?'

'Sure, have you got a stick or disc?'

Chris searched in her bag. She found an official police data stick and handed it over.

'Just the cash machine video,' the guard asked.

Chris nodded.

The guy was white haired but didn't look as old as his hair. He quickly whizzed through the screens. As he waited for the data to load he asked Chris a question. 'What is this for?' he asked, then added, 'am I allowed to ask.'

Chris smiled. 'You are allowed to ask. Doesn't mean I can tell you.'

There was a ping on the screen, job done. The security guard took the stick out and handed it to Chris.

'That was quick. Thanks for that. We can get back to our murder investigation now,' she said with a wry smile.

The guard's eyes lit up. 'Wow, is this to do with the girl the other night down the road?'

She shook her head. 'Sorry,' she said, 'I've already said too much.'

They walked back to the car. Chris was still smiling.

'You know you have a wicked sense of humour Detective Inspector,' John said.

'Having a laugh gets you through the investigation and keeps you sane,' she replied.

'That only works if you are sane to begin with,' John added.

'Touche,' Field said.

INCIDENT ROOM 16:20

JOHN ROSE followed his boss into the incident room. The rest of the team were all working at their screens, a couple on their phones too.

He watched as Field scanned the detectives, looking for a pretender, somebody not busy at all. John knew the skill to, and he plumped for Alfie Muir. His boss agreed and walked over to his desk.

'I know you are busy Alfie, but this takes precedence. You know what both Andy Murdoch and Joe McQueen look like.' He nodded, and she handed him his prize, the stick with the CCTV on it.

'Right, look back every Wednesday to Friday and let me know if you find either of them are at the cash machine drawing money out.'

'Right away ma'am.'

John knew he was being sarcastic because he knew what the job entailed, watching hours and hours of video. 'Right John,' she said turning to speak to him, 'time to see what our Mister Murdoch has to say for himself.'

INTERVIEW 4 ANDY MURDOCH
AUGUST 08 16:35

Interview with Andy Murdoch. Present are Mister Murdoch, Detective Inspector Chris Field, Detective Sergeant John Rose, Detective Constable Anne Wyper.

D.C. Wyper asked Murdoch if he required a solicitor, he refused.

Field: Now Mister Murdoch, you know why we are here. Do you know anything about the death of Iris Muldoon?

Murdoch: Not until you turned up at the flat today.

Field: You didn't find it funny she has been missing for over 4 months?'

Murdoch: Well, I suppose I did a bit, but she told me she was going to stay with a friend in Glasgow.

Field: A woman who is practically a recluse disappears out of the blue for months and you only think it a wee bit funny. It would appear you were the only person she told about this trip. That would seem to me to be a bit funny.

Murdoch: She didn't speak to many people.

Field: She seemed to speak to you a lot.

Murdoch: No, not a lot. She was a strange woman. Often she would go back indoors if you walked into the close rather than speak to you.

Field: What puzzles me is that she must have got a taxi either to the bus or train station. You never saw a taxi at your door around Easter time?

Murdoch: No. If I had seen her leaving I would have told you.

Field: Of course she didn't leave. While she lay dead in her flat somebody had her cash card and was syphoning money from her bank every week. Right at this moment we have somebody combing through CCTV from the autoteller at Tesco's.

That's not going to be you, is it Mister Murdoch?'

Murdoch: No.

Field: Right, I think that's enough for now. Interview suspended at 16:45

Murdoch relaxed for a moment. 'Can I go now?'

Field smiled. 'Not just yet. Oh, I forgot to ask, did you have a key for Missus Muldoon's flat.'

'No.'

'Have you ever had a key for the flat. Maybe while you were doing work for her?

'No, never.'

'Okay, you wait in here, a policeman will wait with you

in case you need anything. We will talk to you later. If we need

to.'

INCIDENT ROOM
17:00

CHRIS AND John walked into the incident room together. D.C. Myra Painter called the D.I. over first.

'Ma'am, the preliminaries from forensics are in. We may have more than 2 or 3 suspects. They turned up DNA on 6 different sperm samples on the bedsheet and pillows.'

Field whistled gently. 'Busy girl. Do they have any matches from Murdoch or McQueen. Not forgetting our own candidate D.C. Sneddon.'

'Still running those tests.'

'Even with those 3 and George Tate we are still 2 gents missing.'

Natasha Simpson called her over next. 'They have just brought Joe McQueen into the station,' she informed her.

'Good. Let's go and see what he has to say for himself.'

She turned and left with John following.

INTERVIEW NO.5
JOE MCQUEEN
AUGUST 08 17:15

Interview with Joe McQueen. Present are Mister McQueen, Detective Inspector Chris Field, Detective Sergeant John Rose and Detective Constable Anne Wyper.

D.C. Wyper asked Mister McQueen was asked if he wanted a solicitor at this stage and he refused.

> Rose: Mister McQueen, the remains of Iris Muldoon were found today in her flat. What do you know about that?
>
> McQueen: Nothing. Oh no, poor woman. I knew something was up when the officers wouldn't let me into my flat. I thought it was to do with her upstairs.
>
> Rose: When did you last see her?
>
> McQueen: Mrs. Muldoon, it was Easter Friday. I know because it was bank holiday, and I was off work. She was polishing the name plate on her front door. She joked about going out to roll her egg on the Sunday.
>
> Rose: She didn't mention about going to stay at a friend over Easter.
>
> McQueen: No. Missus Muldoon never went out now.

Rose: So, where do you think she has been all this time?'

McQueen: I rarely saw her; thought she was still at home, and I just missed her.

Rose: I heard you were in Germany for the Euros. How could you afford that?

McQueen: I saved up since the last World Cup. I couldn't afford to go to the games then, so I decided to save up in case they made it to Germany.

Rose: So, if I check your bank account it will show your savings?'

McQueen: No, I don't like banks. I keep my money in cash in the flat.

Rose: That's not a very safe.

McQueen: Mum said bank managers are all robbers, so I keep cash.

Rose: Did you see a taxi over the Easter weekend at the flats to pick up Iris Muldoon?

McQueen: No. If she went in a taxi I never seen her.

Rose looked over at Field who just shrugged.

Rose: Interview terminated at 17:05

John Rose and Chris Field left the interview room, Joe and stayed there with a police constable who went in the room when they left.

D.I. FIELDS OFFICE 17:15

BACK IN Field's office they both sat quietly.

'What about the unasked question?' John mooted.

The Detective Inspector, the lead on the investigation, looked at the ceiling for a moment. 'You mean serial killer.'

John never spoke. He didn't have to.

'Let's hope the press don't get to this before we have something to give them.'

John checked his phone for local Kilmarnock news.

'Nothing yet,' he said, relief in his voice.

'Where do we go next?' Field asked.

'Obviously the person taking money out of Muldoon's account is key. Murdoch probably wasn't earning much from his DIY. His wife said he was about the flat often. Then there's McQueen. Somebody told me he was at the Euros in Germany, that would cost a pretty penny.

The smoking of cannabis could be key. Who smoked it? I know I smelt it in McQueen's bedroom. Could it be coming from outside as he claimed? Cannabis isn't cheap, especially if they are regular users.'

'Possibly. Couldn't smell it off either today,' Chris said.

'Bet there is hardly a household where somebody has at least tried smoking weed at some time in their lives. Have you?' she continued.

'No,' John said. 'I played football when I was a teenager, the last thing you ever thought about was smoking cigs much less anything stronger.'

Chris laughed. 'Your teenage times were a lifetime ago.'

'Yes, but after that I just never thought about it.'

'Well, I can tell you, you aren't missing much.'

'You like a smoke?'

'We all need something to relax.'

'Bad news boss, you just became a suspect.'

'Tell you what, I might need a smoke, but I really need food now. Have you told your wife you would be late?'

'Yes. Told her I would grab something here. Tell you what, why don't we nip out just now. We can go to Bar XX. I need another word with the owner, Lynne Murdoch. She said Rosie had a fling with a taxi driver, she was going to get me his name.'

BAR XX KILMARNOCK 18:00

JOHN ROSE opened the bar door and let Chris walk in first. The bar was relatively busy, it looked like all the punters were younger than the 2 cops. The only other person near to their age was the owner Lynne Murdoch who walked over to greet them.

'Do you have any news?' she asked.

'No, actually we are here for food,' John answered.

'Sure, take a seat anywhere. I will bring the menus over. Just basic pub grub I am afraid.'

'Sounds good,' he said.

Chris walked over to the table coincidently John sat at earlier with Lynne.

'Food smells good. I could murder a vodka,' Chris said.

'Maybe shouldn't say murder in here,' John whispered.

'Oh Christ, never thought,' Chris said as she put a hand to her face.

Lynne walked over with menus and cutlery. Setting them on the table she sat down next to John and handed him a slip of paper.

'That's the taxi driver's name and the cab co. I also found out one of my barmen took her home one night. His name and number is on there too.'

'Thanks Lynne.'

'Right, shout me over when you know what you want,' she

MR JAMESGLACHAN

said and left them to ponder the menus.

INCIDENT ROOM 19:15

MOST OF the detectives were in the room waiting for the next arranged meeting. There was a second whiteboard placed next to Rosie Baker's with Iris Muldoon's name written at the top.

After their food they returned to the incident room and Chris had written up the little facts they knew, body in freezer, cash withdrawals and neighbours written as suspects.

'Firstly, and very importantly I want no mention of there being a serial killer or the fact the 2 are connected. Until we have evidence of that they are separate. No doubt the press will latch onto it but everything about the murders is completely different. Okay, I know you are all filing reports, but I want to know from each of you where we are,' Chris addressed the team.

'Alfie, have you got anything on the CCTV from the cash machine at Tesco's?' Chris asked.

'Yes. Joe McQueen goes to it every Thursday or Friday but never on a Wednesday.'

The Detective Inspector looked interested with that info.

'We also have Andy Murdoch every week on either a Wednesday, Thursday or Friday.'

'Could you prepare a video of him on a Wednesday withdrawing money?'

'On it now. Should be finished by the time the meeting is over.'

'Great. George, did you get any hits from CCTV or Ring doorbells?'

'Yes, but it's not very encouraging. There is a clear image of Rosie and Colin Sneddon walking along Dundonald Road. The only images we got from Barbadoes Road are from a Ring doorbell across the road. There are a few men walking alone in the direction of the flat in the early hours of Monday. I have sent a copy to forensics to see if they can enhance any of the images.'

'Thanks George. Better result than driving past. That's a learning point for all of you if you need it. Natasha, what do you have?'

Natasha stood up. 'I have been pushing forensics, but they can only go as fast as their machines. Latest estimate is 12 o'clock tomorrow.'

'Nothing else we can do with that then. Myra, what do you have?'

'Update from Digital forensics. List of texts and calls by 12:00 tomorrow.'

'Thanks Myra,' Chris Field said, then looked at John Rose. 'John, you have something to pass on.'

'Yes, spoke to Lynne Murdoch and she gave us another 2 folk we need to speak to. We have a Robbie Allen, who is a local taxi driver and Danny Lewis who works part-time at Bar XX. Anybody free to chase these 2 up. I have their phone numbers, if you could get them in first thing tomorrow morning for a wee chat.'

One of the other detectives stuck up an arm. John had been told his name when he was introduced to them. Unfortunately, as far as he was concerned he was instantly forgettable. He walked over and handed him the slip of paper Lynne had given him.

'Right, John, get the laptop from Alfie. We need to talk to Andy Murdoch again.'

Alfie Muir waved a hand at the boss. 'Ma'am, I would like

to sit in on this one.'

'Okay, bring the laptop with you.'

INTERVIEW NO.6
ANDY MURDOCH

Interview with Andy Murdoch, present are Murdoch, Detective Inspector Chris Field, Detective Sergeant John Rose and Detective Constable Alfie Muir. August 08 19:25

Field: Do you require the services of the duty solicitor or your own one?'

Murdoch: No.

Field: Mister Murdoch, we recently told you about somebody was using Iris Muldoon's bank card to withdraw money from the cash point at Tesco's West Shaw Street on several occasions. Was that you?

Murdoch: No, I told you before.

Field: I am going to show you a video from the store's CCTV.

Alfie Muir plays the clip and shows it to Murdoch.

Murdoch: Of course that's me, but I was withdrawing money for myself with my own card.

Field turns and looks at Alfie Muir, who reads from a
piece of typed paper.

Muir: You also used the card on Thursday 4th April, Wednesday the 10th and 17[h] April,

	Friday 26th April, Thursday 2nd and 9th May, Wednesday 16th May.
Field:	We will get your bank to provide details of your withdrawals. It won't be until tomorrow, but its okay, we will give you a bed for the night.

Murdoch: Stop. I want to speak to a solicitor.

Interview terminated at 19:30.

INSPECTOR FIELD'S OFFICE 18:40

'WHAT'S YOUR feel now John?' the boss asked.

'We have him bang to rights for Muldoon. Don't think he will cop for both even if he did both.'

'Think we will be back in before 21:30?' she asked.

'No, nearer to 22:00 I would think.'

'Probably right. Think we go to the press after that if he admits it. Want to volunteer?'

'First rule of policing, never volunteer. Second rule, let the boss do her own dirty work.'

'Fair enough, you need to hurry home to your waiting wife, all I have is an empty cold house waiting for me.'

INTERVIEW NO.7
ANDY MURDOCH

Interview with Andy Murdoch, present are Murdoch, his legal representative Ben Dorsey, Detective Inspector Chris Field, Detective Sergeant John Rose and Detective Constable Alfie Muir. 21:45 on Thursday 8th August.

Dorsey: I will read out a prepared statement from Andrew Murdoch. After that he will answer no comment to the rest of your questions.

On the 2nd of April I entered the flat of Iris Muldoon. I found her on the kitchen floor, she was dead. When I went to use her phone to call the emergency services I saw her bank statement and saw she had nearly £10,000 in it.

I was struggling for money at the time and when I found her bank card in her purse with a slip of paper with her pin number on it I went to the local Asda to try the pin. When it worked I decided to hide her body. With her being so small she fitted in the freezer.

I admit using the card on multiple occasions, but I did not murder Iris Muldoon and had nothing to do with the murder of Rosie Baker.

Field: Does your wife know about this?

Andy Murdoch looked at Dorsey.

Murdoch: No.

Field: Do you know anything about Rosie Baker's murder?'

Murdoch: No comment.

Field: What were you doing with the money? Were you paying Rosie Baker for sex?

Murdoch: No comment.

Field: Was she blackmailing you?

Murdoch: No comment.

Field: John.

Rose: DNA from more than one male has been found in Rosie Baker's bed. Will your DNA be found there?

Murdoch looked at Dorey. He gave a slight movement

of his head.

Murdoch: No comment.

Field: Okay, this concludes the interview. We will speak again when charges are prepared. Interview terminated at 22:05.

INCIDENT ROOM 22:15

JOHN ROSE and Chris Field walked through the now empty incident room into the boss's office. Alfie Muir had gone to make himself a coffee after the Murdoch interview, the others had all been excused and had gone home.

'Well, that wasn't the result I was expecting,' Chris said as she sat down behind her desk.

'I think he was telling the truth, I think that was what really happened. We will need to confirm she died of natural causes obviously. I think we charge him now with theft. When we find out how Iris Muldoon died we add further charges then if we have to.'

Chris nodded. 'Exactly what I would have suggested. Okay, I will write everything up for the Procurator Fiscal. You head home. I think it's only Alfie Muir that's still here, send him home to.'

'For once I won't argue with you.'

THE ROSE HOUSEHOLD, IRVINE.
09 AUGUST 2024 04:15

JOHN'S MOBILE chirped into life.

'Who is texting you at this time?' Karen grumbled, angry at being roused from her beauty sleep.

John pressed it into life. 'Oh, it's from Chris, my new boss.'

'You aren't going to work at this time, are you?'

John checked his phone's screen. 'No. Just got word from the Fiscal service, we can charge Andy Murdoch with theft.'

'What does that mean?'

'We found a body in a freezer yesterday. He has been charged with taking money from the deceased woman's bank account with her bank card.'

'Dirty rotter. Why has he not been charged with murder?'

'He said she died of natural causes. We won't charge him further until we get the postmortem results back.'

'When will that be?'

'Don't know. They need to wait until she thaws out. Day or 2 probably.'

'So why text you at this time?'

'Says she has been up all night; I will be in charge of the investigation tomorrow until she comes back in.'

'Right, I am going back to sleep now,' Karen said as she turned over and pulled at the covers.

INCIDENT ROOM 08:00 09 AUGUST

JOHN ROSE stood in front of Iris Muldoon's whiteboard.

'In case any of you don't know, last night Andy Murdoch was charged with theft. It being dependent on the postmortem on the victim when it can be carried out before we know if he will be also be charged with murder.

That is also the reason the Detective Inspector isn't here. She stayed on until 5 o'clock this morning. '

One of the phones rang in the office. Alfie Muir walked over and answered it. John waited until the call was finished.

'Sir, that was the duty sergeant, didn't see you coming in this morning. Just wanted to tell you that when Joe McQueen was released last night he was crying when he left the station.'

John put a hand to his chin and rubbed his face. To him that could mean relief just at being released or because he thought he was getting away with murder.

'Right, let's all follow up with the lines of inquiry we have been on. What about Robbie Allan and Danny Lewis?' John said.

John looked expectantly at the detective he still couldn't put a name to. Before he could answer Alfie Muir intervened.

'Sir, that was the other thing the desk sergeant said, there are 2 men in the waiting room. They must be Allan and Lewis.'

'Okay, we can get onto that next. Alfie, you can come with me. Right, George Tate, I want him back here.

Anybody got anything to add?'

Nobody had so he walked away from the whiteboard and headed out, Alfie Muir following quickly behind.

John popped his head round the waiting room door.

'Okay, who was first?'

A tall bald man with a quite imposing figure stood up and walked forward without saying anything. If he had been second John reckoned the other guy wouldn't have protested about the queue jumping anyway.

They walked silently along to the interview room. They still hadn't spoken until they were seated around the table in the interview room.

'I take it it's Mister Allan,' John asked. Although it seemed obvious Lynne wouldn't employ the guy as a barman. Bouncer maybe.

The big guy just nodded.

'Right, this is just for elimination purposes. But we will be recording it to make sure our notes are exact.'

John nodded to Alfie to kick things off.

INTERVIEW NO. 8
ROBBIE ALLAN

Interview with Robbie Allan. Present are Mister Allan, Detective Sergeant John Rose and Detective Constable Alfie Muir. 9th August 08:15 hrs.

Alfie Muir asked informed Mister Allan that although it was an informal interview he could have the services of a lawyer at that time, he declined.

Rose: Mister Allan I assume you know why you are her. How do you know Rosie Baker?

Allan: I have known her for over a year. She works at Barr XX, in the town centre. The owner pays to get her staff taken home at closing time of the pub.

I have often driven her and the other staff home.

Rose: Worked Mister Allan. I am sure you know she was murdered on Monday morning, that is why you are here.

Allan: Sorry, slip of the tongue.

Rose: You know why you are here; we have been told you slept with her. Was it just the once?

Allan: Yes. A week past Thursday night it was. She wanted dropped off last when I took the staff home. She was on a bit of a downer; I told her how shit my life was and she invited me into her flat.

Rose:	What contact did you have with her after that?
Allan:	She phoned me a couple of times.
Rose:	Just a couple? We will get her phone records shortly. They don't lie and I would advise you not to. It will save us time and you bother if you stick to the truth.
Allan:	Well, it was more than a couple of times. Truth was she was becoming a phone pest. Eventually I told her not to call me again but then I had to block her. She was asking my workmates to pass messages to me, eventually I had to call Lynne at the Bar XX and get her to have a word with her.
Rose:	Where were you in the early hours of Monday morning, say between 1 and 3 o'clock?
Allan:	Well, here is where there is a coincidence, you see there was a party on at the pub just down from Barbadoes Street. My taxi is for pre-bookings, not a hackney where I can just pick up people off the street, so I parked up in the Tesco's which is very near the pub. If people phoned I could be there in a couple of minutes.
Rose:	I think I know the pub you mean. Is that the pub and restaurant on the corner? Would Lidl's car park not be nearer?
Allan:	It is that one, yes. The thing is if you park that close you get folk banging on your windows wanting you to take them home, when you refuse they can get nasty.
Rose:	Tesco's car park is very near Rosie Baker's flat. So, how long were you parked up for?
Allan:	Well, the thing is when I stopped there just after 1 o'clock I felt knackered. I was nightshift

on the previous 2 nights, and I hadn't slept much that day. I must have drifted off to sleep, next thing I know one of the other drivers is knocking on my driver's door window. He thought I had taken ill.

Rose: What time would that have been then?

Allan: It was 5 to 3. I was pig sick; I had lost a lot of possible hires because of it.

Rose: How would you describe Rosie Baker's emotions toward you.

Allan didn't answer.

Rose: Infatuation.

Allan: Possibly. Probably.

Rose: Did she want you bad enough to threaten to tell your wife?

Allan: No. Look, I said it was over and that was that.

Rose: She phoned you 3 nights in a row, that doesn't sound like she wanted to give you up. What if she threatened to tell your wife. You and her weren't getting on, what would happen if Rosie told her about you and her. You would need to stop her, shut her up before she did that.

Allan: No, none of that is true.

Rose: From what I was told about her Rosie Baker was the kind of girl who took no for an answer. She used her wiles to get her way.

Allan: Look, I didn't know her that well. We had sex once, nothing else.

Rose: Did you do that often, have sex with fares?

Allan: No, she was the only one. I've had a couple of blow jobs from birds that didn't have the fare

	home over the years. That's it.
Rose:	Strange then that Rosie was the only one you had sex with. I think that's very strange. So, while Rosie was being murdered you were conveniently asleep behind the wheel of your taxi less than 100 yards away.
Allan:	It's true. I was asleep.
Rose:	Very convenient. One more thing, do you smoke cannabis?
Allan:	What and drive a taxi? No way, it's not worth the risk.
Rose:	Could you get some cannabis if you wanted to?
Allan:	I suppose so.
Rose:	Right, I think that is enough for this morning.
Muir:	Interview terminated at 08:40.
Allan:	So, what happens now?
Rose:	We look into everything you said and what everybody else is saying then we might need to speak with you again. Oh, and we will need your mobile phone and a DNA sample.
Allan:	What, for how long? I need it for my livelihood.
Rose:	It will be a couple of days while the digital forensics in Glasgow interrogate it. If you hand it in to the desk sergeant he will make sure you get it back as soon as we are finished with it.

Allan got up and stood intimidatingly, just staring at John Rose, as if he wanted to say or do something to him. Instead, he just turned and walked out.

'Take him to the desk sergeant then get the next one Alfie. Make sure Robbie Allan hands his mobile in and has a DNA sample done,' John said with a smile.

INTERVIEW NO.9
DANNY LEWIS

Interview with Danny Lewis. Present are Mister Lewis, Detective

Sergeant John Rose and Detective Constable Alfie Muir. 9th August

at 08:55.

Muir:	Mister Lewis, although this is an informal interview you may request the services of a lawyer if you wish.
Lewis:	No, I have nothing to hide.
Rose:	Glad to hear it. Now you know why you are here. How did you know Rosie Baker?
Lewis:	I knew her from work, although I didn't know her that well.
Rose:	You knew her well enough to sleep with her.
Lewis:	It was just the once.
Rose:	When was this?
Lewis:	Let me think, it was a week past on Wednesday.
Rose:	So, what happened?
Lewis:	The taxi didn't turn up. There was only Jan Todd, Rosie and myself on that night. Jan phoned the taxi, and they said it would be ¾ of an hour before they could get to us. Jan was keen to get locked up so I offered to walk Rosie home.
Rose:	So, you walked her home.

Lewis: Yes. I was feeling a bit horny that night, so I gave her a bit of the patter and she invited me in, and we ended up in bed.

Rose: After that?

Lewis: She didn't mention it again, so neither did I.

Rose: Were you not disappointed. A fine young hunk like you, she didn't compliment you, didn't ask you up again?

Lewis: Maybe you are too old to know what it's like nowadays.

Rose: Like what exactly?

Lewis: Sex and love and all that, they don't necessarily go like that.

Rose: How often do you have casual sex then? Every night, every few nights?

Lewis: Just whenever.

Rose: So, can you account for your whereabouts in the early hours of Monday morning, between the hours of 1 and 3 o'clock.

Lewis: I was in my bed.

Rose: Where do you live?

Lewis: I live with my parents. They have a house in Fairyhill Road.

Rose: Is that near to Barbadoes Road? I don't know the geography of Kilmarnock that well.

Muir: Conveniently sir, it's the next street down the road.

Rose: Were your parents at home on Sunday evening?

Lewis: No, they were away for the weekend.

Rose: Were you home alone or did you have another one-night stand with you?

Lewis: No, Mccaulay Culkin was with me.

Rose:	Listen son, you might think this is a joke but it's a murder investigation. Right now you are a suspect. You know go to jail, do not pass go.
Lewis:	Sorry.
Rose:	Did you leave the house between 1 and 3 o'clock in the morning?
Lewis:	No.
Rose:	Did you smoke cannabis on Sunday or Monday?

Lewis stalled.

Muir:	You aren't going to get into trouble by admitting it to us.
Lewis:	Yes, I had a few spliffs.
Rose:	Okay, Danny, that's it for the moment. We will be in touch if we need anything else from you. Oh, and we will need your mobile phone and a DNA sample before you leave.
Muir:	Interview terminated at 09:15.

John and Alfie walked Danny through to the desk sergeant and left him there before heading back up to the incident room.

'Alfie, what's the name of the guy who was checking for CCTV and Ring doorbells?'

'Garrett, sir.'

'Thanks, looks like I have another wee job for him.'

INCIDENT ROOM 09:25

D.C. MUIR OPENED the door and let his superior walk into the room first.

John walked over to D.C. Garrett. 'George, I have a wee job for you. I know you like looking for CCTV stuff, I want you to head to Barbadoes Road and walk round to Fairyhill Road looking for any recordings on the Monday morning from 1 o'clock and say 5 o'clock to be sure.'

'Who or what am I looking for?'

'Anybody. It seems folk are queuing up to be suspects.'

Garrett took the jacket from the back of his seat.

'Sir, is it okay if I drive down to Barbadoes Road?'

'Yes, George. As long as you walk the route when you get there.'

George smiled as he left the office.

Natasha called John over next. 'Sir, the forensic report and autopsy are both here.' She stood up and handed him printed copies of both.

'Thanks.' He took them and walked over to his desk.

First he looked at the full autopsy report. Rosie was killed by strangulation. The marks on her neck were consistent with a length of electrical cable or similar being used. There were also marks where she had been clawing at her neck trying to save her life. Nothing else was different from what they had heard at the postmortem and the only surprise was the presence of cannabis in her bloodstream which they already knew about.

The forensic report showed the presence of sperm in her vagina which was expected to be their colleagues although John wondered if there was anybody else's there too.

As far as residual DNA was concerned there was so much on her face and shoulders that it would not be possible to isolate any. There was also no sign of where the murder took place although it wasn't believed to be in the bedroom.

John threw the report on his desk. 'Think John,' he whispered to himself. Who wanted her dead. Also, who had the strength to choke her so hard by pulling a piece of cable.

He took out his notebook and wrote all the 6

suspects names down. Then he put ticks against them.

'Sir.'

John looked up and saw Natasha Simpson standing in front of him. She looked over to the notes he was scribbling.

'Iris Muldoon's postmortem is scheduled for 09:00 tomorrow morning.'

'Thanks Natasha. No doubt I will be going along with the D.I. You could join us if you want.'

'Are you just looking for a driver?' she asked with a smile.

'No. It will be unique. For all my years in the force I have never been to a postmortem where the body has been frozen.'

'Gosh, yes. I never thought of that. Sure, I will go with you. I will be driving no doubt.'

'Well, if you are offering,' he said, as she turned and walked back to her desk.

John looked down as his note. There was something he missed. He looked over the autopsy report again.

Half way through the report he clicked his fingers. Why had he missed it? No doubt the droning of the pathologist had made him miss the fact, but he had already read through the report thoroughly and missed it again.

Tissue damage is more pronounced on the right side of the neck pointing to more pressure being applied by a person who is either left-handed or has a stronger left arm.

John added left-handed to the notes he had.

Alfie Muir was next to disturb him. He walked over, However, he didn't catch John unawares as his squeaky shoes meant he signalled his arrival.

'Sir, we have a print-out of Rosie Barker's phone calls and texts for the last 2 months.'

John looked and saw the Detective Constable was holding a bundle of sheets of printed paper.

'Okay, give me the texts. Are you okay to go through the calls?'

Alfie handed the file for the texts. John pulled lucky, it was only a quarter of the size of the phone calls.

Alfie winced. 'Yes, but there is a lot here.'

'Okay,' John said, then stood up. 'Anybody spare at the moment?'

Myra Painter put up a hand, then stood up.

'Alfie, get together with Myra. Split the bundle and go through them separately. When you are finished compare notes for your report.

When Alfie walked away John started looking through the texts, starting with the latest that was on the Monday morning at 01:05 from George Tate.

ROSIE MY HEART BROKE SINCE WE BROKED UP NEED TO SEE YOU CALL ME XXXXXXXXXXXXXXX

John Rose shook his head. What was a nice girl doing with a numbskull like Tate.

The next message was sent by Rosie on the Sunday night at 22:05.

ROBBIE, PLEASE PHONE ME. I MIGHT BE PREGNANT R.

John couldn't believe what he had read. What he Needed to know was had Robbie Allan read it. He called Alfie Muir over.

'What's the number for the mobile forensics?'

'Why?'

'I need to know if this text has been read.'

Alfie shook his head. 'Don't think they can help. If it was a Whatsap you would know, but if hers was not an iphone you can't tell. Hers definitely wasn't. I saw it.'

'Okay, thanks Alfie.'

John looked back through previous texts. Sure

enough, starting from Monday after they slept together there were over a dozen texts to Robbie's number. No mention of pregnancy, just that she needed to see him again.

If he did see the message on the Sunday then he had a major motive to kill.

John skimmed through the rest. All pretty mind-numbingly boring until he found the texts from George Tate, obviously after they split up. Tate started off denying any wrongdoing then changed to begging for forgiveness, all of which Rosie staunchly rejected.

Natasha Simpson stood in front of John again.

'Sir, Joe McQueen is downstairs, says he has something you need to know.'

'Why doesn't the front desk not phone me?'

'They have been phoning the D.I.'s phone.'

'Okay, I will go down and see him.'

John walked down and found a nervous looking McQueen sitting in one of the waiting rooms.

'Hi Joe. You have something to tell me.'

'Yes. I just remembered that on Monday morning, just as I was leaving for work there was a lot of shouting upstairs.'

'Where from, do you mean, from Rosie's flat?'

'No. The Murdoch's. They argue a lot, but this was really

loud.'

'What time was that then?'

'I leave the flat at 7 o'clock.'

'Was Shona not nightshift?'

'Don't know. It was really bad. She was calling him all sorts of names.'

'Like what?'

Joe shrugged. 'She called him a dirty bastard, whoremaster, you know things like that. she said I bet it's that whore you were with.'

'Who did she mean?' John asked.

'I looked up and she was pointing to Rosie's room, but Rosie isn't a whore. That's it really. Just thought you would want to know.'

'Of course, they didn't tell us they argued. Right, well thanks for that Joe. Anything else then let us know. You can phone if you want save you coming in. Have you still got one of our cards.'

'Yes. There was something else. About 5 o'clock this morning there was shouting and screaming from their flat. I opened the flat door and was going to go out and see what was wrong when Andy came storming past me. He was holding his face and it was bleeding. I asked him if he was okay, and he told me to fuck off. Then Shona appeared at the top landing and told him not to ever come back to the flat.'

'Well, thanks for coming in. As I said you could have just phoned.'

'It's okay, the lorry is just round the corner. So, did Andy kill Mrs. Muldoon?'

'Why, what have you heard?'

'Nothing, but you let me go then Shona threw Andy out.'

'No. Our enquiries are ongoing. That's all I can say at the moment.'

'Okay'

'Right, come on, I will show you out.'

John sat down back at his desk. So, Shona Murdoch accused Andy of having an affair with Rosie. He didn't want her knowing he had been in her flat, maybe he did more than help her with her electrics. Then he obviously confessed he was stealing Iris Muldoon's money. They would need to talk to Andy again that was for sure.

John was walking past the front desk after he showed Joe McQueen out when the officer called him over.

'Sir, is Detective Inspector Field not in?'

'No, not just now. She was here until 5 this morning. Why?'

'Detective Chief Inspector Church has been calling her office and mobile numbers all morning. He wants to know what's happening with the 2 murders.'

'I am on extension 87, could you ask him to call me in 5 minutes,' John asked.

'Okay, sir,' she said, then turned and headed for the door to the back office.

John walked back up the stairs and back to the incident room. When he got to his desk the phone was already ringing.

'D.S. Rose,' he answered.

'Church here. Where is Field? She is supposed to update me every morning.'

John could sense the latent anger in his voice.

'Sorry you weren't told; Chris Field was here until after 5 o'clock this morning. We don't expect her in until 13:00, sir.'

'Well, she should have delegated somebody to contact me.'

'I will say to her when she comes in. We got a good result yesterday.'

'Well, I think you should get me up to speed. I have been trying to find out all morning.'

'The Rosie Barker case is growing arms and legs, if you will pardon the expression. We currently have 6 suspects and we don't know if any more will appear. As you must have heard we found the body of Iris Muldoon her freezer in the flat on the ground floor of the same block as Rosie Barker's.'

'Two bodies in the same close. Sounds like we have a serial killer,' Church said.

'We don't think so. Andy Murdoch has said he found the woman, who was in her 70's, dead from natural causes. He hid her body in her freezer then started syphoning money from her bank account, and he has been charged with that.'

'John, I hear what you are saying but you can't believe 2 deaths from the same block of 4 aren't just a coincidence. I don't know about you, but I don't believe in coincidences.'

'No sir, neither do we. However, until they can carry out a postmortem on Mrs. Muldoon we won't know if it is murder. No point in jumping to conclusions. Chris spoke to the procurator and the feeling was it would be thrown out.'

'Why has the postmortem not been scheduled for today?' Church asked, his patience sounded as if it was growing thin.

'Sir, it's scheduled for tomorrow morning. They have been waiting for the body to thaw out. She had been stuck in a freezer for nearly 5 months.'

'Okay, I want an update from one of you tomorrow as soon as the postmortem is complete. Clear?'

'Clear, sir.'

The phone went dead.

John looked at the silent receiver before dropping it back in its cradle. Ignorant twats like him reminded John why he had signed up for the road to retirement.

He went back to checking the text messages that had been downloaded from Rosie's phone.

Dead on 12 noon the door to the Incident room opened and Detective Inspector Chris Field walked in carrying a large box.

'Right folks, Greggs time,' she said, causing everybody to stop what they were doing and walk over for their share.

Chris put the box down on a table, keeping a

carrier bag to herself as she walked towards her office.

'John Rose was the only person who neither stopped working or interested himself in the boss' freebies. However as Chris passed his desk she stopped.

'Ours is in this bag John,' she said and nodded towards her office. 'I need to know what's new.'

'You are early. Didn't expect you here for another hour,' John said in his way of welcoming. With that he got up and went round his desk and followed his boss into her office. He hadn't felt hungry until Chris got his roll out of the bag opened it, filling the room with distinctive, lovely and unmistakable smell of bacon.

'Got them sausage rolls, we got the good stuff,' she said before tucking into her own roll with gusto.

There was silence for a few minutes as they ate hungrily.

'Anyway, when you are awake and have nothing to do at home then I am as well coming in to annoy you lot. So, what's new?' Chris said as she picked at a bit of trapped bacon at her back teeth.

'Bad news first. D.C.I. Church wasn't happy he didn't

get an early morning update.'

'Chris sighed. 'My bad,' she said. 'Forgot all about it.

Anyway, when is he ever happy?'

'Don't know. I mean I know who he is but apart from passing him in the corridor in Saltcoats nick a few years ago I've never really met him. Seemed to be a bit of a pompous prick on the phone. Hung up on me to.

We got Rosie's phone records. I have been looking through her texts. She receives a message from George Tate at 01:05 on the Monday morning, asking her to phone him. More interestingly she sent a text to Robbie Allan at 22:05 on the Sunday night saying she could be pregnant.'

'Waw. Yet according to the postmortem she wasn't. Could be he got spooked with the text and decided to keep her quiet.'

'Yes, could be. Talking of the postmortem the finished report is in. Found something interesting, appears the killer was left-handed as the tissue damage on the right-hand side of her neck was greater than the left-hand side.'

'What do we know of the suspects, what hands are their strongest? '

'Not something that came into the equation until today, boss. Oh, and speaking of postmortems, Iris Muldoon is at 09:00 tomorrow. Our esteemed boss wants a phone call as soon as it is over.'

'Think we should have an update meeting at 13:00 then John?'

'Yes, good idea. The other thing that happened today, Joe McQueen dropped in. Told me that on Monday morning Andy and Shona Murdoch had a blazing row, she accused him of having an affair with Rosie. They were also rowing this morning when he got home from here. Think he confessed all to her.'

'Sounds like it.'

'Right John, fudge doughnuts next. Hope you like, but I don't really care if you don't, I love them.'

'Sorry boss, I am partial to them too.'

INCIDENT ROOM 13:00

CHRIS DELEGATED meeting leader to John, who stood at the Iris Muldoon whiteboard first. 'Right folks, firstly a big thanks for the Greggs from the D.I. If you get stuck into the case the way you got stuck into the food it will be solved later today.'

This got both a laugh and a cheer from the assembly.

'Right, Iris Muldoon first. As you know Andy Murdoch was charged last night, or more correctly this morning, with theft from the victim's bank account. As you know it could be construed as fraud, but the prosecution service wanted us to deem it theft. There could be further charges for him, we will find out after the postmortem is at 09:00 tomorrow. The results of which will determine what, if any further charges he will face.'

John then moved back to the Rosie Baker's whiteboard.

'This morning, we got the postmortem and forensic reports

and the details from Rosie's phone including calls and texts. How many of you have read anything of either, or both, postmortem and forensic reports?'

John looked round and saw 3 detectives had read something of them. 'Disappointing. I know you are all busy but you should take even a few minutes to skim read the reports even if you don't have time to commit to reading them all.

Most significant thing I found from the pathologist's report is that he thinks the killer is either left-handed or has a stronger left hand. We will need to find out from all the suspects which arm they favour when we re-interview all suspects.

From the forensic report it has identified all 6 suspects as having deposited sperm on Rosie's bedclothes. Having sex with somebody doesn't necessary mean they would murder them, but from other background information there is enough to have them all as suspects.

I have been going through the texts Rosie sent and received. She received a text from George Tate just after 1 a.m. on the Monday morning asking her to phone him. Did he phone her?'

John looked to Alfie Muir and Myra Painter as he

didn't know how they had divvied up the calls.

'Sir, the only call she had after midnight that she answered was after 7 a.m., from a number that can't be traced.'

'Well, if the phone tech experts can't trace it what chance do we have. The other text of interest was one she sent to Robbie Allan just after 22 :00 on the Sunday night where she said she was pregnant. According to the postmortem she wasn't pregnant. Did Robbie Allan want her out of the way if she was carrying his child? Over to Alfie and Myra, what do you have from the calls?'

The 2 detectives looked at each other before Alfie stood up first.

'Sir, apart from the call I told you about the only thing I found was that she bombarded Robbie Allan's phone with calls. It was 8 within an hour at one stage. For 2 days she called him constantly then stopped altogether. Apart from that, nothing out of the ordinary.'

Alfie sat down and Myra took her cue to get up.

'I have logged her calls. Almost all were to and from the

Barr XX. There were a few to George Tate but that stopped months ago.'

'What about videos or pictures, was anything reported about them?'

Alfie stood again. 'Sir, they sent a printout of the photos she had taken. Mostly they were selfies or pictures with other bar staff or friends. The only ones that included a male were ones of her and George Tate which were all dated months ago.'

'Okay, anybody with anything to add?' John Rose asked.

'D.C. Myra Painter stood. Sir, the DNA results from Rosie's bedsheets are in.' With that she walked over and handed John a printed sheet. He looked at it, whistled then held it over to Chris Field.

'Okay folks, let's keep working on what you are on and make sure everything you find is recorded. If you don't record it, it never happened.'

John joined Chris who was smiling.

'You have a cheek,' she said quietly.

'Oh, you were warned about me. Hate writing reports, but you know that.'

'Right, I better give D.C.I. Church a call, get you in the clear of any blame.'

'Okay, but you don't need to. I will keep going through the
Rosie's texts. The needle in the haystack might be there.'

CROSSHOUSE HOSPITAL MORGUE
10 AUGUST 08:50

Natasha Simpson managed to get the police car parked in the vicinity of the Morgue although the hospital car park was busy, even for that early on a Saturday morning. All 3, Field, Rose and Simson walked together, neither looking forward to what lay ahead. Frozen, defrosted or whatever state the corpse was in there would still be the smell. An indescribable smell but absolutely horrible just the same. When they walked into the viewing area there was already a woman sitting taking notes. John didn't know who she was, but Chris didn't look happy to see her. The pathologist, a different one from Rosie's postmortem, stopped what he was doing when he saw the 3 take their seats. 'Nice of you to join us. You have missed almost the first 30 minutes so I will recap.'

Chris looked at John then they both looked at Natasha who shrugged.

The pathologist continued. 'Having examined the body, apart from some slight skin damage, no doubt being caused by being forced into the freezer, there is no obvious trauma. No bruising, contusions or broken limbs.'

He continued with his work explaining to them all, and the other woman watching in particular, what he was finding. An hour later he was finished. He declared that everything pointer to Iris Muldoon had died through natural causes, almost certainly from a heart attack.

As they got up Chris thanked the pathologist and they turned to go out. After Chris and Natasha walked out John looked back and saw the woman, who John tagged as a journalist, talking to the pathologist.

As they walked down the corridor John asked Chris who the woman was.

Chris leaned in and whispered, 'that is Fionagh Hamilton.'

'Journalist I take it.'

'Yes. She was on the path to being a big shot in

London
but her career suddenly floundered. Rumour was she was hitting
the bottle. Anyway, she is back where she started, at the
Kilmarnock Standard. They are linked to the Daily Record now and
she sees that as the way back to the big time.'

'I take it she is looking for a scoop,' John said.

'No, character assassination is her speciality. Anyway, I
could murder a coffee. Let's go to the café.'

'Are you going to phone Church first?' John asked.

'I think the D.C.I. can wait half an hour.'

Behind them they heard the rapidly approaching clip-
clopping of no doubt expensive high heels. The 3 cops stopped
and Fionagh Hamilton walked past, slowing her pace to offer
them a look of distain.

After she passed they were hit by a big whiff of very
expensive perfume.

'She has enough of that on,' John said quietly.

Chris Field snarled, 'probably to mask the smell of
vodka. 'I'd love to smack that bitch,' she added.

John and Natasha laughed, but their boss didn't. She
was deadly serious.

Natasha didn't join them in the coffee bar and waited in

the car for them. Twenty minutes later John and Chris joined her.

'You missed a treat, Natasha,' Chris Field said, smiling.

'Better than the muck in the canteen. That was proper coffee.'

Field was disturbed by her phone ringing.

'The boss,' she said, looking at the screen before answering. 'I was just going to phone you,' was all she got out before there was an explosion of verbals from the other end of the phone.

John and Natasha looked on as the colour drained from her face. After a minute or so of uninterrupted barracking Chris put her hand over the phone and mouthed- 'check Kilmarnock Standard online.'

The other two quickly googled the on-line newspaper and stared at the lead article.

KILLIE SERIAL KILLER by Fionagh Hamilton

Kilmarnock residents are living in fear after 2 bodies were found in a block of flats in Barbadoes Road this week.

Police Scotland have released no details of the incident leaving terrified neighbours scared to leave their houses as the serial killer walks the streets among them.

Chris finished her call, and John handed her his phone.

'Fucking Fionagh fucking Hamilton,' Chris said. 'I just fucking wish I had seen this before she passed us in the corridor,'

'It was only published 30 minutes ago,' Natasha chipped in.

Chris laughed. 'After all that I didn't get to tell Church that Iris Muldoon had died of natural causes.'

'So, apart from the bollocking what did he say?'

'We will soon find out; he is heading in to headquarters for a meeting with us.'

INCIDENT ROOM 11:00

EVERYBODY WAS in the Incident room, quietly waiting
when D.C.I. Church walked in. Everybody stopped what they were doing and turned to face him.

'Not much work going on here,' was his opening line,
After walking into the room and standing in the middle, looking
round and making eye contact with everybody. Then he turned and
looked directly at D.I. Field.

'So, where exactly are we?' he asked.

'We attended the postmortem this morning and the
conclusion was that Iris Muldoon died of natural causes,' she said.

She was standing behind D.S. Rose who was seated at his desk.

'So there does not appear to be a serial killer,' Church
said.

'No sir.'

'What of the Rosie Baker investigation, do we

still have 6 Suspects or has there been any increase overnight?'

'No sir, still just the 6.'

Detective Chief Inspector Colin Church then pointed to D.C. Myra Painter. 'Inform the press officer I will be holding a press conference at 17:00 hours tonight.' Then he turned to the Detective Inspector again. 'I will be informing the press that there is no serial killer in Kilmarnock and that the 6 suspects in the Rosie Baker murder have been arrested and are helping us with our inquiries. Do I make myself clear?'

'Yes sir,' Chris Field said.

'Is everybody in agreement?'

'Yes sir,' echoed around the room.

'I will get every available detective in Ayrshire here to help and even beyond if I have to will be here to assist.'

With that, he said 'carry on,' then headed out.

John turned to Chris. 'Did he really say and mean arrest them?'

'You heard the man, same as I did. Arrest them he said and arrest them we will.'

'You know what that means?'

'Yip, we will be practically living here for the next 48 hours.'

She then turned to the other detectives who were mostly chatting to themselves. 'Well, you heard the man, lets get on with it,' Chris Field said.

INCIDENT ROOM 15:00

DETECTIVE INSPECTOR Chris Field walked out of her room and walked up to John Rose's desk.

'Update.'

'Sneddon is making his own way in. Murdoch, McQueen and Robbie Allan are either here or on their way. The other 2 are presently uncontactable.'

'Right, get everybody available out looking for Lewis and Tate.'

John stood up. 'In case you didn't hear, anybody who is available get out and track down Danny Lewis and George.'

Three of the detectives got up and readied themselves to go out.

'What about extra bodies,' Chris asked.

'We have 3 coming from Ayr and 2 from Saltcoats.'

'Right, I have readied the press release for Church and sent it to him. No doubt he will rewrite the lot, but he asked for it. Right a coffee then we start interviewing again.' Her mobile burst into life again. 'Not Church again,' she said before answering.

This time she didn't get to speak before her boss launched into another tirade.

She nodded to John, and he followed her into her office. As she sat behind her desk and brought up the Kilmarnock Standard news page again. All the time Church was still continuing with his diatribe.

When Church stopped talking they looked at a photo of them both appeared on the computer screen.

'I will kill that fucking bitch, John,' Chris said.

Their picture, which was of the 2 of them in the hospital cafe
was under the heading-

KILLIE COPS COFFEE WHILE KILLER AT LARGE

by Fionagh Hamilton.

D.C. Field and D.S. Rose, so called "top cops," relax at a coffee shop while the killer of Kilmarnock woman Rosie Baker walks freely on the streets of Kilmarnock.

'Fucking bitch. I see she is sticking with the gh after her name.
Probably wants to forget she is just plain Fiona and from Kilmarnock.'

'Why did she do that?' John asked.

'There is a real big shot journalist in London, The Times I think.
When she landed down in the smoke she was told she couldn't use her own name. Anyway, better forget the coffee, let's go and rip these suspects new arseholes,' Chris said.

'Still, it was a good coffee,' John said, and they both laughed.

INTERVIEW NO. 10
JOE MCQUEEN

Interview with Joe McQueen. Present are Joe McQueen, solicitor Irene Green, Detective Inspector Chris Field, Detective Sergeant John Rose and Detective Constable Natasha Simpson. 10th August 15: 20.

Field: Mister McQueen, you have been charged with the murder of your neighbour Rosie Baker.

McQueen: I didn't do it.

Field: You can say that until you are blue in the face, but you have lied to us. Semen with your DNA was found on the bedclothes from Rosie's bed. You told us you have never been in her flat. If that was true, how did it get there?

McQueen's lip started trembling and tears filled his eyes.

McQueen: I've been a bad boy.

Field: What did you do?

McQueen: Rosie was expecting a parcel one day. She told me her key was on a string in the letterbox. What I have done in the past is wait until everybody is out and I go up to her flat and go in. I smell her dirty panties and imagine we are doing it.

Field: Is that it? You have had 3 days and that is all you came up with. Come on Joe, give us the truth.

McQueen: It's true, I am a virgin. I have never had sex. I loved

Rosie but I would never harm her.

Field: So why was your sperm on the bedclothes?

McQueen: Sometimes I would do it onto the pillows. I thought if she smelled my stuff she would fall in love with me.

Rose: Joe are you right or left-handed?

McQueen: Right.

Rose: How strong is your left arm?

McQueen: Not too good. I broke it 2 years ago; it's never been the same since.

Field: Okay, we will take a rest now. Interview ended at 15:38.

INTERVIEW NO.11
ANDY MURDOCH

Interview with Andy Murdoch. Present are Mister Murdoch, Solicitor Ben Dorsey, Detective Inspector Chris Field, Detective Sergeant John Rose and Detective Constable Natasha Simpson.

August 10th 16:00.

Field: You have been charged with the murder of Rosie Baker. If you continue with no comment answers we will think you have something to hide, so it is in your best interests to tell us all you know.

Did you murder Rosie Baker?

Murdoch: No.

Field: Do you know who did?

Murdoch: No.

Field: Did you know there was a key inside her letterbox?

Murdoch: No.

Field: You told us you were in the flat on at least 1 occasion. Did you not see the key then?

Murdoch: No. Maybe she put it there after that day, I don't know.

Field: Sperm with your DNA was found on the bedclothes in Rosie's bed. How did it get there?

Murdoch: Will my wife find out about this?

Field: Only if it comes to court. If you are innocent then it won't.

Murdoch: I told you before I went into her flat because her electricity was tripping. That was true. When she came to the flat door she had been doing her hair when the power tripped. I went in and told her to switch her hairdryer and straighteners off.

Then I told her to put one on at a time. I followed her into her bedroom. She leaned down in front of me. She was wearing a nightie and had no bra on, that was clear to see. When she leaned down I saw she wasn't wearing pants either.

I must admit I was turned on. We traced the fault with the electrics to a faulty pair of straighteners. She offered me a coffee and we stood in the kitchen drinking it. As I said I was turned on at the fact she had no pants. I chatted her up, saying I hadn't seen her boyfriend about, she said they split up. I asked her if she missed him, she said the biggest thing she missed was his cuddles.

I offered her a cuddle and she took me up on it. We held each other tight, and she felt my hardness. She said to me that I must be missing having sex with my wife being pregnant. I said I was and if I was being honest I was getting desperate She led me by the hand through to her bedroom.

That was it. We had sex that one time and it was never mentioned again.

Field: Did you not find it strange?

Murdoch: What strange?

Field: That she never offered? From what we know Miss Baker knew what she wanted and made sure she got it.

Murdoch: Obviously she didn't want me.

Field: What did you and your wife quarrel about on the Monday morning when she arrived home from work?

Murdoch: I was at the pub watching the football on Sunday night. I got drunk and fell asleep at a friend's house.

Field: What is the friends name?

Murdoch: My wife definitely won't find out about this.

Field: As I said earlier, not if you are innocent.

Murdoch: You see, it was at a friend of hers flat. She is called Rose Warnock.

Field: Where did you sleep? On the couch, spare room?

Murdoch: No. I slept in her bed, although i didn't sleep much. I didn't get home until 3 o'clock.

My mobile was out of battery and Shona had been phoning the landline. She thought I was ill, or something had happened to me. She came home early from her shift, when she saw me she exploded.

Went berserk, accused me of sleeping with Rosie and having an affair with her.

Field: Why did she think you were having an affair with Rosie?

Murdoch: It was her reputation.

Field: Reptuation?

Murdoch: You couldn't help but notice it, different guys coming and going at all times of the night. At one stage Shona though Rosie was on the game.

Field: Is that why you stormed away from the flat?

Murdoch: Yes, when she goes off on one like that the best thing to do is get away from her and wait until she calms down.

She phoned me later and said it was her hormones and

it was okay now.

Field: John, anything you want to ask.

Rose: Did your wife hit you?

Murdoch: No. she went to pushed me away. When I put my hand up to stop her, her hand hit my face and gave me a nosebleed.

Rose: Is she ever violent with you?

Murdoch: No. We used to have playfights, but that stopped when she got pregnant.

Rose: One more thing, what hand do you write with?

Murdoch: I am left-handed.

Rose: That's all from me.

Field: Interview terminated at 16:30

Field and Rose left the interview room and headed for the desk sergeant, hoping for good news. Before they got there P.C. Neil Ross, the police rep. who was sitting for Colin Sneddon, intercepted them.

'Why has Colin been arrested?' he asked.

'Take it up with the D.C.I., his orders, not mine,' Field answered.

'This isn't the procedure.'

'Take it up with the D.C.I., not what I would have done, but he makes the decisions around here, not you or me.'

'When are you interviewing him then?'

'Let's go for 17:00, if that's ok with you.'

'We are ready now.'

'Okay then,' Field said, 'let's make it 17:00.'

The desk sergeant smiled as they approached his desk.

'This is the busiest Saturday we have had for a while.

This shift has flown in.'

'Glad to hear it. What about Tate and Lewis?' Chris asked.

'Lewis is here, Tate is in a car on his way here,' the desk sergeant replied.

'Thanks,' she said with a smile of relief.

Then she turned to John Rose. 'Right, quick debrief in my office.'

D.I. FIELDS OFFICE 16:40

CHRIS SLUMPED into her chair. 'It's been a long day already,' she said. 'Four more to go at least. What do you think about those 2?'

'You know over the years I have always had a nose for the truth, been a major part in me being a good detective. This lot have me perplexed. Joe McQueen isn't very clever, but I think he is too stupid to lie, if you know what I mean.'

'Not really, but carry on,' the D.I. said.

'Murdoch. We will need to follow up on this Rose Warnock, see if his story holds up. What I don't get is if Rosie was obsessed with Robbie Allan why did she not bother the same with Andy Murdoch who was practically on her doorstep or any of the others?'

'Could be a woman thing. Maybe the others had b.o. or bad breath or was just shit in bed? Maybe Robbie Allan had a big cock. Think I will ask for proof when we interview him later.'

'I thought size didn't matter,' John said.

'Sure, that's what all the guys with wee willie's say. What do you say?'

'I am taking the fifth on that, boss,' he said, and they both laughed.

INTERVIEW NO.12
D.C. COLIN SNEDDON

Interview with Detective Colin Sneddon, present are Sneddon, P.C. Neil Ross, Detective Inspector Chris Field, Detective Sergeant John Rose and Detective Constable Natasha Simpson.

10th August, 17:00.

    Field: Okay, Colin, you know the ropes, tell us about Sunday night, Monday morning.

    Sneddon: As I said before, I was in the Bar XX with a couple of mates. They were down because Killie got pumped by Celtic. What made it worse was we expected the team to give them a game, but they were rubbish. So my mates went home before 11. I was off on the Monday and stayed, hoping for a bit of action.

                  George Tate, who used to be Rosie Baker the barmaid's boyfriend turned up at the bar, trying to get off with her again. Just after that one of Rosie's pals turned up and told her Tate tried to get off with her. When Tate came back from the toilet Rosie told him to sling his hook. When he left he threatened her.

    Field: What, did he say to her?

    Sneddon: Nothing, he just made a gesture. I didn't see it but she sort of freaked out. Anyway, I thought I had a chance with her, and I knew of her reputation.

Field:	What reputation was that?
Sneddon:	Well, it was well known she was easy. You know, liked the men. So, anyway, I tried it on, you know to calm her. Told her I was a copper and that if she needed protection I would help her. At the end of the night, it turned out the taxi was running late and I offered to walk her home. So, I walked her back to her flat and she invited me in. We had sex then I left her.
Field:	Where was she when you left her?
Sneddon:	She was lying on the bed.
Field:	Did you have a smoke?
Sneddon:	What do you mean a smoke?
Field:	For God's sake Colin, don't come the innocent. In case you forgot this is a murder investigation. Now, did you, or her, or both of you smoke anything legal or illegal?
Sneddon:	No. We went in, went to her bedroom, had sex then left.
Field:	Did she contact you again?
Sneddon:	No. I never thought anymore about her until the Wednesday when we went to her flat.
Rose:	Are you right or left-handed?
Sneddon:	Right, but I have a very strong left hand. I played in goals when I was young. They did a test, and it turned out my left arm was stronger than my right.
Field:	Anything else John?
Rose:	When you left the building did you close the front door, you know the main door to the block?
Sneddon:	Yes. It was locked when we got there, so I made sure it was secure when I left.

Rose: When you left did you see anybody hanging around. Loitering, or did you pass anyone on the street?

Sneddon: No. The streets were very quiet. Passed a couple heading home from somewhere, that was all.

Field: That's enough for now. Interview terminated at 17:12.

INTERVIEW NO.13
ROBBIE ALLAN

Interview with Robbie Allan. Present are Mister Allan, his lawyer Robbie Mason, Detective Inspector Chris Field, Detective Sergeant John Rose and Detective Constable Alfie

Muir. August 10th 17:30.

Field: Mister Allan, how do you know Rosie Baker?

Allan: We have been through all this before.

Field: Sorry, but I thought it would get your brief up to speed.

Allan: I have been driving the staff of the Bar XX home for years. Rosie is one of the barmaids. I know her from that.

Field: So, what has happened since your little liaison you told us about?

Allan: She phoned me continuously to the point I blocked her. I contacted her boss and told her.

Field: You said you were parked in Tesco's car park until 3 o'clock on the morning Rosie was murdered. We have checked the store's CCTV and there is a taxi there, but it appears empty.

Allan: No way. I was sitting in the driver's seat asleep. I was wearing dark clothes, maybe that was why they couldn't see me. One of my colleagues woke me at

	3 o'clock. Thought I was ill because it took ages to wake me.
Field:	Where you are parked is on the edge of the car park there were shadows next to you. You could easily have got out of your cab unobserved and gone to Rosie's flat.
Allan:	I suppose I could have but it was the last thing I would do. She was a pest.
Field:	What do we do with pests Robbie? Eradicate them.
Mason:	Come on Detective, my client has answered all your questions truthfully. The fact he was parked less than a mile from where Miss Baker was murdered is a coincidence.
Field:	Sorry, Mister Mason but I don't believe in coincidence.
	Now Mister Allan, did you receive a text from Rosie on Sunday evening saying she was pregnant.
Allan:	Yes I got it. I laughed for ages.
Field:	I wouldn't find it a laughing matter.
Allan:	Well, I did, I have had the snip. Shooting blanks, so if she is pregnant it isn't mine.
Field:	I thought you blocked her calls.
Allan:	All right, the truth is my wife, and I, haven't been getting on. I hadn't had sex for weeks. Rosie was the last person I had sex with. I toyed with going round for another, you know, for sex. That was why I unblocked her, but I didn't go to see her though. As I told you I fell asleep.
Field:	John.
Rose:	Mister Allan, are you right or left-handed?
Allan:	What?
Rose:	Simple question left or right.

Allan:	Left, but I don't know why you are asking.
Rose:	You have a good physique; do you go to the gym?
Allan:	Yes, try to go twice a week. Why, what's this about?
Field:	Mister Allan, in a police interview it is us that ask the questions. Interview terminated at 17:42.

D.I. FIELDS OFFICE 17:50

'BETTER CHECK the papers, see how Church's press conference went down,' Chris said.

Before John sat down he joined her behind her desk and watched over her shoulder as she quickly brought up the Kilmarnock Standard first. She banged her hand on the desk as the main headline came on the screen.

KILLIE C.I.D THINK WE ARE ALL SUSPECTS

By Fionagh Hamilton

Kilmarnock C.I.D. are chasing shadows in the hunt for the murderer of 23-year-old Rosie Baker.

At least 6 men have been arrested today including one of their own, a Detective Constable who we are not at liberty to name. This unprecedented move smacks of desperation from a force run by underachieving detectives.

'She has a bit of a point,' John said. 'Arresting 6 people, Church has made us all look stupid.'

'No, John, it's me she is after. Did it before, that was how she got her big move before.'

'That's news to me,' John said.

'It was when I was a Detective Sergeant. She found out that I was having an affair with a married senior officer. Worse, and I didn't know it, but his wife was dying of cancer.'

'Oh God.'

'He didn't help either. I was left to cop it, if you pardon the pun. Took me years to rebuild my career and here she is trying to do it again.'

'Speaking of being left to take the flack, where is our esteemed D.C.I.'

'Oh, he is away for the rest of the weekend.'

'Never mind that, I think we need food,' John said. 'What do you fancy, Chris?'

'I don't fancy Chinese or Indian, nothing like that.'

'What if I phone Bar XX, see if they do takeaways, I can nip round and get it. Or we can go round there for the next photoshoot.'

'Funny, but you won't get me to laugh. Yes, see if we can get burger and chips.'

John dialled the number. Lynne eventually answered.

'Hi Lynne, it's John Rose. I was wondering if you do

carry outs? We are stuck here in the station on Rosie's case and
are looking for 2 burgers and chips. I will come round and pick it
up if you could oblidge.'

'We don't usually do carry outs, but for you anything.
Give me 15 minutes and they will be ready for you.'

'Cheers, thanks Lynne.'

Chris smiled when he killed the call. 'She fancies you,'
she said.

John wished he hadn't made the call with his phone's
speaker on. 'Fancies me? I am a married man,' he scoffed.

'Come on, don't say you haven't seen the signals?'

'I haven't been looking for any signs or signals. I think
we have enough to be going on with here. Anyway, I better head
round there. Unless you want to go?'

'No, she doesn't fancy me. I will get these,' Chris said,
reaching for her handbag.

'No, you can get the breakfasts,' John said as he got up
to leave.

BAR XX 18:15

JOHN WALKED into the bar and found it as expected for a Saturday night, busy, loud, rowdy. Everybody in good humour. The Tunes blasting and there was football on the big TV screen.

Lynne was behind the bar and waved to him when he walked in. John walked over, struggling to get through the crowded passageways, wary of spilling anybody's drink.

Lynne beamed a smile. 'Nice to see you again,' she said, when the music hit a quiet spot.

John walked over to a quiet spot at the end of the bar and Lynne moved over towards him.

'Food won't be a moment,' she said.

'Why did you not tell me Robbie Allan complained to you about Rosie pestering him?' he asked her.

'Better come through to the office.'

John weaved past the 2 barmaids who were busy sorting drinks.

Lynne told John to close the door behind him and the noise

level dropped dramatically. Still a buzz in the background, but at least they could talk without shouting.

Instead of going behind her desk Lynne stood in front of John. They were so close he could smell her perfume, almost taste it.

'The thing is John; Rosie was more than a barmaid to me. She was more like the daughter I never had. I don't want people to think the worst of her. She was a sweet girl, innocent in a way, but wouldn't listen to me where men were involved.'

'It was just because we were interviewing Robbie today and he said it. Threw me a bit because I thought you would have mentioned it, that was all.'

'I'm sorry, I didn't think it was important,' she smiled and moved a bit closer to him. 'When this is over I hope you pop in sometime for a drink and a chat. I know it's been strange circumstances, but I feel I can talk easily to you, you know very easily.'

She moved closer again. Her body was almost touching against his. She licked her lips.

There was a knock on the door behind John.

'Lynne, the takeaway food is ready,' the muffled voice announced.

Saved by the knock, John thought for a second, then Lynne leaned forward and kissed him. On the lips. Forceful, putting the tip of her tongue in when he didn't object.

One kiss, then she broke off and moved back, letting him open the door.

John moved out and an older woman, who must be the cook, handed him a paper carrier bag. John pulled a £20 note from his pocket and turned to hand it to Lynne.

'No need for that, it's on us, for all the work you are doing, a way of saying thanks,' she said, then added, 'for now.'

As he had walked past John had noticed a bucket on the bar with Rosie's picture on it and a notice saying the collection was for her burial and memorial. John threw the note in the bucket as he passed.

He left the bar without looking back to see if Lynne was watching him leave.

INTERVIEW NO.14
DANNY LEWIS

Interview with Danny Lewis. Present are Mister Lewis, his lawyer Debbie Golder, Detective Inspector Chris Field, Detective Sergeant John Rose and Detective Constable Alfie Muir. 10th August 2024 at 19:10

Field: How do you know Rosie Baker?

Lewis: She works, I mean worked beside me at the Bar XX. Oh, and I shagged her once.

Field: When was that?

Lewis: About 10 days ago.

Field: Just the once you said. Couldn't have been very good then.

Lewis: She was all right.

Field: I meant you.

Golder: Inspector Field, this is a murder inquiry. I think you should be taking things more seriously.

Field: Sorry. So, what were your movements on the early hours of Sunday morning?

Lewis: A few of my mates were round in the afternoon to watch the football. We had a lot to drink, and a few spliffs, I ended up in bed early. Didn't get up until 9 o'clock the next morning.

Field: We know your parents' house is the next

street to Barbadoes Road where Rosie lived. We have a CCTV image of you at 2 am walking down Barbadoes Road on the opposite side of the street from Rosie's flat. How do you explain that?

Lewis conferred with his brief before answering the question.

Lewis: To tell you the truth, I might have walked down Barbadoes Road at that time. I woke up and needed a fix. Don't even know what time it was. Anyway, my mate lives down that road, honestly I was probably still off my tits at that time.

Field: There is no other CCTV of you until an hour later when you passed back that way. It wouldn't take an hour to walk down that road and back with what you were going to smoke. Would it?

Lewis spoke to his brief again.

Lewis: No comment.

Field: Mister Lewis, your brief might be advising you to say that, but in my eyes not speaking is tantamount to admitting guilt.

Lewis: It's not that, the guy who gives me the weed works with my father and he could lose his job.

Field: Well, I am sure that's more important than being charged with murder, like you have been.

Lewis conferred again.

Lewis: His name is Ian Burton, he lives almost directly across the road from Rosie's flat. When I went to his I had a smoke there.

Field: Why did you not tell us all this at your first interview. It would have saved us and yourself

	a lot of bother.
Lewis:	Sorry, but it is true.
Field:	Which hand do you write with?
Lewis:	My right, why?
Field:	It's called background information. I think we can end the interview here. Interview terminated at 19:25.

INTERVIEW NO. 15
GEORGE TATE

Interview with George Tate, present are Mister Tate, Detective Inspector Chris Field, Detective Sergeant John Rose and Detective Constable Natasha Simpson, 10th August at 19:45.

Simpson: For the recording Mister Tate could you confirm that you were offered the services of a duty solicitor, but you refused.

Tate: Yes, I don't need a brief, I didn't kill her.

Rose: You aren't being interviewed under caution this time, you have been charged with murder.

Tate: Unless you lot are fitting me up I have nothing to worry about.

Rose: George, you know we don't do things like that.

So, let's go back to Sunday night. You went to the Bar XX pub at what time?

Tate: Think it was about half past 10.

Field: How long were you in there?

Tate: About half an hour at the most.

Field: You weren't happy that Rosie took the drink she bought you and poured it down the sink.

	What did you say to her?
Tate:	It was her mate's fault. She told her I tried to get off with her in a pub across the road.
Field:	Did you?
Tate:	Yeah. Well, I didn't know she was Rosie's mate. I had never met her before.
Field:	More than one witness has said you turned round before you left and did a gesture with your hand across your throat, as if you were going to kill her.
Tate:	What? No. Who told you that? Her pal was blitzed and most of the others at the bar were sozzled too.
Rose:	One of the witnesses was bar staff and hadn't been drinking and the other was an off-duty policeman.
Tate:	Oh, here it is, the set-up. Maybe I do need a brief.
Rose:	You were also seen leaving the block of flats where Rosie lived around 2 a.m. and walking up past the block, away from the main road. Where were you going at that time?
Tate:	It wasn't me he saw. I was tucked up in bed with Sta, Christ, I nearly said it there.
Rose:	George, if you don't get your witness to corroborate things and provide you with an alibi then the murder could be pinned on you.
Tate:	No way, I want a lawyer now.
Rose:	One last thing before stop to organise a lawyer. Are you left or right-handed.
Tate:	Left, why?

Nobody said anything to him.

| Tate: | Right, that's it, I want a lawyer. |

Rose: Interview terminated at 20:00.

D.I. FIELDS OFFICE 20:10

'WELL JOHN, what would your plan of action be now?' Chris Field asked.

'I would leave them all to stew overnight. We go home and get a good nights rest, ready to start again in the morning.'

Chris stroked her chin. 'Sounds inviting.'

'I did mean we go to our own homes,' he said, laughing.

'Really? I thought you might be heading to the Bar XX?'

'What? Why do you say that?'

'Well, I have never seen tomato ketchup that was cherry red colour.'

'It wasn't like that. She went to kiss my cheek, I wasn't expecting it and I turned round. It was innocent enough.'

Chris turned and looked out the window. 'No flying pigs, John.'

Before John could reply Chris clapped her hands together.

'You are right, John, your suggestion sound like a plan, let's all go home. If any of the 6 wants to confess the duty sergeant will give me a call at home.'

THE ROSE RESIDENCE 07:15 AUGUST 11^(TH)

'DON'T FORGET to be here at 2 o'clock or don't come home at all!' Karen reminded John for the umpteenth time.

He was in the hallway ready to leave when his wife had called out from the bedroom upstairs.

'Two o'clock sharp, I know,' he called back to her.

It was his daughter's 30th birthday and they were giving her a voucher to spend on a holiday. He was under orders to be back home at 2 on the dot. No ifs, no buts.

As John drove to Kilmarnock, he remembered what he got from his parents for his 30th, a card with a tenner in it. Not a voucher for well over a grand. Changed days.

INCIDENT ROOM 08:00 AUGUST 11^(TH)

DETECTIVE INSPECTOR Chris Field took the morning meeting. Everybody was drinking either coffee or tea, desperate to be alert for the long day ahead they were all expecting.

'Okay folks, we have an update, and we are about

to release 3 of the suspects. George Tate has an alibi, Stacey
Hill walked into the station last night and gave a statement
saying George was with her.'
This brought a reaction from all the people who
knew Stacey, or more importantly she was the bidey-in of
Dan 'snuffer' McGeachy. If he found out about Tate dipping
his girl jail would be a pleasure.
'Danny Lewis was given an alibi by his mate Ian
Burton and he can go and thirdly Andy Murdoch was
vouched for by Rose Warnock. The other 3 will be
interviewed again this morning with the new evidence we
have about them.'

INTERVIEW NO.16
JOE MCQUEEN

Interview with Joe McQueen present are Mister McQueen,
his lawyer Irene Green, Detective Inspector Chris Field, Detective Sergeant John Rose and Detective Constable Natasha Simpson. August 11th 08:30.

Field: Mister McQueen, how many times have you gone into Rosie Baker's flat.

McQueen: I don't know.

Field: Once, twice, twenty times? What is nearer?

McQueen: Maybe about 10 or 20.

Field: When was the last time?

McQueen: Not last weekend, the weekend before.

Field: Did you masturbate that time?

McQueen: Yes. I did it on her pillow.

Field: Right, Joe, the thing is, the young man who was with her on Monday morning says he definitely closed the close door when he left, and she was alive when he left. We all know there is no way anybody could get in through the buildings back door because the walls on all three sides of the back gardens are over 8 foot tall and the back door is kept bolted shut. So, that leaves me thinking the person who went into her flat and murdered her needed to be in the building.

Now, Andy and Shona Murdoch were both out, we know Iris Muldoon was dead so that just leaves you in the building.

Joe started crying.

Green: I think my client and I need a break.

Simpson: Interview suspended at 08:45 hrs.

McQueen and his brief left the interview room. The others stayed behind.

Field: Well, I think he is about to crack.

Rose: I think he has cracked, but not because he is a murderer. Boss, he is low intellect. Whatever he is, I don't think he is a murderer. What's your view Natasha?

Simpson: Think I agree with you, Sergeant.

Rose: My experience tells me he has done something he shouldn't have, like the wanking, but definitely not murder.

Field: My money is on we get a statement in half an hour.

Rose: Right, bet you he is out before lunchtime, which you are buying.

Field: You are on.

INTERVIEW NO. 16 JOE MCQUEEN continued. 09:15.

Field: Are you ready to continue Joe?

McQueen: Yes.

Field: Why were you upset Joe?

McQueen: It was just thinking how terrible it was that somebody would murder Rosie. She was so beautiful.

Field: You heard the front door close, what did you do next?

McQueen: I. I. I went up to her flat and knocked on the door to make sure she was all right.

Field: Was she?

McQueen: Yes. She said to me, what did you forget. Then she saw it was me. I said do you want a smoke. She said her landlord said she couldn't smoke in the flat. I said I won't tell him if you don't. She laughed. She looks prettier when she laughs. Anyway, we smoked our joints then I left.

Field: Did you touch her?

McQueen: No.

Field: Did you have sex?

McQueen: No.

Field: Did you ask her for sex? Did she knock you back? Spurn your advances.

McQueen: No. I wouldn't have sex with her until we were married. But she wouldn't marry me.

Field: So, after you smoked you left.

McQueen: Yes. She kissed me on the cheek. I went down the stairs. When I got to the flat door I heard the front door being unlocked. I hurried in and looked through the peephole in the door. It was Andy.

Field: What time was that?

McQueen: Just about 3 o'clock. I remember looking at the time when I went in.

Field: What did you do then?

McQueen: I watched porn then fell asleep on the chair.

Field: Earlier you said you saw Rosie's ex-boyfriend leaving the flat. Was it definitely him?

Joe whispered to his Irene, his lawyer. Are you sure, he whispered when she gave him advice.

McQueen: No, it wasn't him.

Field: Why did you say it was him?

Joe didn't answer.

Field: Joe, why did you say that?

McQueen: I wanted him to get the blame. He didn't treat her nice. I would have treated her better.

Field: Who was it then?

McQueen: A young guy. He is a Killie fan; I have seen him at the games. He was wearing a Killie jacket.

Field: Right, I think that's enough for now. Interview terminated at 09:33.

D.I FIELD'S OFFICE 09:40

'WELL, I THINK Joe is innocent,' Chris Field said.

'Yes, I agree,' John Rose said. 'Bet you Colin Sneddon will be sick when he realises he was in the frame because Joe wanted to drop George Tate in it.'

'It was his own fault for having sex out of marriage,' Chris said and managed a straight face when she said it.

'Are you serious,' John said. 'We all did it.'

Chris couldn't keep her face straight any longer. 'Of course I am joking, but it was him thinking with his nuts instead of his nut that got him in the brown stuff.'

'He will be glad to be out and back in the team.'

'No, he won't be involved with us until the whole investigation is over. The defence would have a field day if they found out he was involved.'

'Of course, I wasn't thinking. So, what do we do about Joe McQueen, Chris? If we let him go we only have Robbie Allan left?'

'Let's interview Robbie Allan first, then we can decide.'

'Yes. Let's do it. Oh, by the way I need to be home for an hour or so this afternoon. Daughter's 30th birthday and if I don't be there at 2 o'clock I won't have any nuts to think with.'

'Sure, after we interview Robbie Allan we will need to see what else the team have dug up to see where we go next.'

INTERVIEW NO.17 ROBBIE ALLAN

Interview with Robbie Allan. Present are Mister Allan, his
lawyer Robbie Mason, Detective Inspector Chris Field, Detective Sergeant John Rose and Detective Constable Natasha Simpson. August 11th 10:00.

Rose: Mister Allan, you said you were parked on Monday morning between 1 and 3 a.m.

Allan: Yes.

Rose: You were parked there for quick access to the party nearby.

Allan: Yes.

Rose: Then why did you switch your phone off?

Allan: I didn't.

Rose: Robbie, your phone was interrogated by our digital forensic specialist. It was off. Why did you have it off?

Allan: I needed a sleep. I haven't been getting any sleep at home. The wife and I aren't getting on and we just argue all the time.

Rose: You see, the way I see it, you were parked at a place where you could sneak out and go to Rosie's flat. She was pestering you all the time. One of your fellow taxi drivers told us she was pestering them for your home phone number and address. You weren't getting on with your wife, what would happen if she found your home address. You had to make sure that didn't happen.

Allan: If she turned up at my home the wife would batter her. She was just a stupid wee lassie.

Rose: What about after she left? Your marriage would be over. You had to eliminate her, didn't you.

Allan: I am not a murderer. I've never laid a finger on a woman, not in my nature that.

Rose: What about her message from Rosie about being pregnant, that must have scared you.

Allan: No. I told you; I have had the snip. I am shooting blanks.

Rose: Funny, but there is nothing on your medical records about that.

Did you think we wouldn't check your medical records?

Allan:	Well, the truth is, I did her up the arse. I didn't want to mention it before.
Rose:	Chris, do you have anything you want to ask?
Field:	There is an image of somebody who resembles you we took from a Ring doorbell on Barbadoes Road at 2:35 am on Monday morning across the road from Rosie's flat. It is currently with forensics to try to improve the image. If it is you how would you explain it?
Allan:	Not me. If he looks like me it's just a coincidence.
Field:	Mister Allan. I don't believe in coincidence.
Rose:	We will speak again when we get the new image back. Interview terminated at 10:25.

D.I. FIELDS OFFICE 10:35

'TELL YOU what John, if Robbie Allan didn't do it he isn't helping himself.'

'Can't disagree with you. However, if he did it we don't know how he got in the building,' John asked his boss.

'Maybe Andy Murdoch didn't close the door fully.'

'Possibly, that was just after he came home. There is still something about this that doesn't add up to me. You know, something at the back of my head says we are still missing something.'

The office phone rang. Chris answered it and smiled. The smile got bigger, and her eyes brightened. She put the phone down and said 'yes!'

'What?' John asked.

'John, there is a God. That was the desk sergeant. Bloke from Green Flag was called out to a puncture repair. The woman stank of drink and called it in.'

John shrugged. He wanted to tell her to get to the

punchline, but she was savouring every second of whatever was tickling her fancy.

'The traffic boys are bringing her in.'

'Who!' John said in frustration.

'Fiona fucking Hamilton, without the gh,'

'No wonder your ecstatic. Bet you are going to see her when she is in the cells.'

'Too fucking right. The girl who dragged herself out of Onthank, made it to the heights in London and is now going to be thankful to be back living in Onthank,' Chris said.

John smiled; he had never seen her so high. He hoped they would be celebrating a similar high shortly when they nailed Rosie Baker's killer.

THE ROSE RESIDENCE 13:55

JOHN PARKED his Audi on the driveway and smiled, he had 5 minutes to spare. During the 10-minute drive from Kilmarnock he was mentally ruminating the aspects of the case as he tried to work out what he was missing.

When he walked in the place was a hubbub, the family and a few friends were there and had obviously had more than a few drinks.

'There's my dad!' Vicky shouted when she saw him. He hadn't even managed to get his jacket on before she was cuddling him.

'You are pissed,' he said.

'No, I've only had 2 drinks,' she slurred.

'What were they, pints of vodka?'

Karen waved him over and she got the envelope with Vicky's present in it. She handed him the envelop, that was a signal for him to do the business.

'Vicky, here's your birthday present. Your mum and I thought you needed a holiday.'

Vicky walked over and took the envelop from her father. She opened it and took out the voucher. 'Oh my God. Oh, this is too much. Kids,' she said to her 2 kids, 'we are going to Disneyland,' and the toddlers shouted for joy.

'Maybe Eurodisney,' her father said.

Vicky kneeled down and hugged her 2 kids.

Karen pulled at John's arm. 'Your dinners in the oven, we've all had ours,' she said. It was meant to be said quietly but the consumed alcohol affected her volume control which meant everybody was looking at them.

'I am ready for it, I've not had anything since breakfast,' John replied.

'What, have you not been for coffee with your boss!' Tommy Brown, one of John's neighbours called out, much to everyone's delight. They all laughed and pointed to John.

Obviously the previous day's news had been the topic of conversation before he arrived. He should have expected to get ridiculed at some stage.

Before John could reply Karen spoke. 'Best of it, is he never takes me for a coffee. No but he will cosy up to his boss. Bet you bought his too.'

'His, Karen John's boss is a woman. Chris Field is her name,' Tommy said again. There was more laughing.

'A woman. You never said your new boss was a woman.'

'No, but I never said she wasn't.'

'Oh, go and get your dinner. We will talk about it when get home tonight. Taking a woman out for coffee.'

'Before I disappear into the kitchen I think we should toast the birthday girl. Has everybody got a drink?'

'No, you haven't!' Tommy shouted again.

A drink was thrust in his hand by his son-in-law and John cleared his throat.

'Vicky, it hardly seems 30 years since we brought you out of the hospital, now that wee bundle of joy has her own 2. We wish you all the best for the year and hope you have a great holiday. To Vicky, Happy 30th birthday.'

Everybody shouted happy birthday while John took

a sip of the drink. It was red wine, his good stuff he had hidden away. He knew the way it burned gently as the little he drank slipped down his throat.

There was plenty left in the glass as he sat it down on the coffee table.

'Right folks, I shall retire to the kitchen and have a bite to eat.'

Even after he closed the kitchen door John could still hear the babble from the living room. He would make a joke as he left not to disturb the neighbours with the noise because both lots of neighbours were at the party.

John looked in the oven and saw Karen had done him proud. It was the family's favourite, steak pie, roast potatoes and peas and carrots.

He took it out of the oven and was surprised it wasn't well-done to the point of charring. Karen had never been good at just keeping things warm, it was either cold or burnt.

He put a bit of the steak into his mouth, and it melted. Everything else on the plate was cooked perfectly and John ate almost greedily. He hadn't realised just how hungry he had been.

He was almost finished when the kitchen door opened.

Vicky walked in and smiled when she saw her father.

'Dad, thanks for this. Brian and I really need a holiday, Are you sure you can afford it?'

'No, we can't. Do you think we can get it back and try and cash it in.'

Vicky looked at him, not understanding he was pulling her leg, obviously because she had swallowed too much booze.

'I am only kidding love. I am due a big payout from

my pension shortly so we can afford it. We will get you some spending when you decide where you are going.'

'Oh, thanks dad,' and she walked over and cuddled him. After she hugged him she said, 'I will leave you to finish your dinner now. It was good, wasn't it.'

'Yes. I am just surprised your mum didn't cremate it.'

'No, I sorted it. The secret is to leave it on a low heat then put the heat off. The residual heat keeps it warm enough.'

Vicky left and John finished what he had left on his plate. As he did he thought about Rosie's death from the beginning. Why was the thermostat turned up? What would that do? He clicked his fingers. It was as if everything clicked into place. Who did it, when they did it and why they did it.

He needed to get back to work.

After his lunch John shouted Karen into the kitchen.

'Listen love, I need to get back to work.'

'Already. You have only been here 10 minutes.'

'The thing is, Vicky just said something to me, and I know who killed Rosie. Sooner I get back the sooner I can get finished. I think it will be another late one though.'

'Well, if you need to go. Better say cheerio to everyone.'

The music was on in the living room and people were chatting above it. John called over the grandkids and gave them big hugs and kisses. He would have loved to have stayed on but now he knew who the murderer was he was desperate to get going on it.

When he put his suit jacket back on Karen killed the music and the room quickly went quiet.

'Sorry folks, but I need to get back. There has been a

development. Hope you enjoy the rest of the day. You will probably all still be here when I get back.'

'Don't be going near any coffee shops!' Tommy called out.

'Oh, on that, there's been a development. Check the papers tomorrow, more likely to be in the Scottish Sun, the Record will try to bury it. My favourite reporter will be in the news for a change.'

As he headed for the door the music went back up and the chatter restarted.

John sat in the car before driving off. He googled a number and phoned. Eventually he got through to the correct department and found out what he wanted to know.

Next he phoned the Detective Inspector and arranged to meet her and another Detective Constable before starting the car and heading off.

CROSSHOUSE HOSPITAL A&E
AUGUST 11, 15:05

JOHN ARRIVED a minute before D.C. Simpson who parked the police car behind his. He got out and met up with her and the D.I..

'What's the plan?' Field asked.

'You and I go in and arrest Shona Murdoch. Natasha you go and check with the CCTV operator. See if Shona arrived on Tuesday night with a large bag. If she does try and find out where she puts it.'

'Are you sure about this John?' his boss asks him.

'Yes. Remember I said about the thermostat being turned up and we wondered why. It was so that when the pathologist examined Rosie's body he wouldn't be able to give an accurate time of death. The person who would know to do that had to be medically trained.'

'Is that it?' she asked.

'No. You said you don't believe in coincidence, well there is more than one here.'

'Okay, on your head be it, but if you arrest an 8-month pregnant woman for nothing there will be Hell to pay.'

'Come on, let's go. Natasha, the D.I. and Murdoch can travel with me, you stick with the CCTV and keep the car.'

'Okay sir,' she said, as she headed in the opposite

direction, heading for the main entrance.

John and Chris headed to the Accident and Emergency entrance.

'Well, did you go down and visit Fiona Hamilton without the gh?'

Chris smiled like the Cheshire cat. 'You bet. The person who said you should never enjoy revenge was an arsehole. She was sitting in the cell feeling sorry for herself. I looked in and never spoke, just smiled.'

The A and E waiting room was busy. John led the way up to the counter and showed his warrant card He said he needed to speak to Shona Murdoch.

They were quickly shown through to the back area, much to the annoyance of the people who had been waiting, some for hours. John could hear the shouting as they closed the doors behind them.

Shona appeared from one of the cubicles, there was blood on her blue gloved hands.

'We need a word, Mrs. Murdoch.'

'Oh, right,' she said, then pulled off the examination gloves and dropped them in a bin.

'How can I help?' she said, smiling.

'Shona Murdoch I am arresting you,' John started saying.

'But Iris Muldoon died of natural causes,' Shona interrupted.

'Rosie Baker didn't,' Field said, before letting John continue.

'For the murder of Rosie Baker. Anything you do say will be used in evidence.'

Shona put her hands out. 'Is this when you put the cuffs on,' she said flippantly.

'I don't think we need them; you aren't going to

make a run for it, are you?' John asked.

'I need to get my bag and stuff,' Shona said.

'It's okay, I will come with you to get them,' Chris said.

INCIDENT ROOM 15:40

JOHN AND Chris walked into the incident room, all heads turned to them.

'Shona Murdoch has just been arrested for Rosie Baker's murder,' Chris Field informed them.

There was silence for a moment while the team looked at each other. Nobody saw that move coming.

D.C. Myra Painter put a hand up. 'Ma'am, we got the enhanced image from the Ring doorbell. It isn't Robbie Allan. In fact, the guy is walking a dog.'

This brought a nervous laugh from the team.

'Natasha Simpson is still at the hospital checking out CCTV. Hopefully she can find the clip we want. We are waiting Shona's lawyer coming in before we can interview her. In the meantime, I think it's safe to let Robbie Allan go.'

She turned to John who just nodded.

INTERVIEW NO.18
SHONA MURDOCH

Interview with Shona Murdoch. Present are Mrs. Murdoch, her lawyer Ben Dorsey, Detective Inspector Chris Field, Detective Sergeant John Rose and Detective Constable Alfie Muir. August 11th 16:30.

Dorsey: Before we start I think considering Shona's pregnancy we limit each session to 15 minutes.

Field: Of course. Her health and wellbeing is very important to us.

Dorsey: Okay. I will time it if you don't mind.

Rose: Shona, you made this murder inquiry very difficult. You really threw us when you turned up the thermostat. You knew that increasing the temperature meant the pathologist couldn't give an accurate time of death. Is that correct?

Murdoch: No comment.

Rose: Only somebody with a knowledge of medicine would know that. Then there was the thermostat switch. It was wiped clean. Another move, the person who murdered Rosie knew about leaving evidence. You knew about forensics it because you studied it at university before going into nursing. That's correct, isn't it.

Murdoch: No comment.

Rose: In any murder there are the w words; who, where, when and why and the h word- how. Who I know, it is you. Where we know but now we are onto why.

Your husband was released because he had an alibi. Did he tell you who gave him it?

Murdoch: No comment.

Rose: The person who gave him the alibi was a friend of yours. A very good friend by all accounts. Bestie you could call her.

While you were working on Sunday night, your husband was in bed with Rose Warnock. He didn't leave her until nearly 3 a.m. Did you know that?

Murdoch: No comment.

Rose: When we interviewed Rose she said she had a strange phone call on Monday morning. The caller withheld their number and simply asked who she was. When Rose said her first name they cut the call. Was that you who made the call?

Murdoch: No comment.

Rose: This is where coincidence comes in. You thought Andy was having a sexual affair with Rosie Baker. When Rose said her name you thought she said Rosie, didn't you?

Murdoch: No comment.

Rose: We have your mobile phone, and we will be interrogating it. Although you withheld your number we can still trace it to your phone.

When you cut the call you were angry. Raging. You had accused your husband of having an affair and found a text on his phone. The text read:

John read from his notebook:

> Hi DIY man, I have a hole needs filling tonight are you available. X

Not very subtle. You thought this message was from Rosie, didn't you?

Murdoch: No comment.

Dorsey: Detective Rose, we know you are due to retire. It looks as though you want to go out on a high, charging a pregnant woman with murder. So far I have heard no solid evidence from you, my client may or may not have had an argument with her husband then may then have made a phone call to a friend. Is that you have?

Rose: No, we have more. However, by getting your client to answer everything with "no comment" does not help us get to the truth. Your stalling interruption is also impinging on the little time you have allowed us to speak to your client.

Mrs. Murdoch, after you phoned Rose, thinking it was Rosie, you decided to end your husband's affair that you thought he was having with your neighbour, who you thought was a slut, by ending her life, didn't you?

Murdoch: No comment.

Rose: Being a nurse and having to lift bodies you are quite strong. You decided to strangle her. You knew just choking her would leave DNA traces, so you used a piece of flex. You knocked on her door, when she started to walk away you threw the flex over her head and pulled it until she was dead. Is that what you did?

Murdoch: No comment.

Shona Murdoch then turned and whispered to her brief.

Dorsey: My client wishes to have a break. She doesn't feel well and would like to see a doctor.

Rose: Interview terminated at 15:42.

D.I. FIELDS OFFICE 15:50

D.I. FIELDS, D.S. Rose and D.C. Muir sat in the office for their interview debrief.

'Well John, I doubted you before, but I think you have come up trumps,' the boss said. 'What do you think Alfie?'

'Yes, guilty all the way. She didn't say much but her face gave up her guilt. Up until you mentioned Rose she thought she had murdered her husband's lover,' Alfie said.

'It's okay knowing she is guilty, we still have to prove it,' John said, putting a slight dampener on the mood.

'Is Natasha not back from the hospital yet?' John then asked.

The D.I. stood up and looked through the window in the office door. She hadn't been in the office when they walked though a minute before.

'Don't see her,' she said then took her mobile out

and called her.

'What's your location?' she asked.

'Just parking up in the car park, be up in 2 minutes.'

'What's the verdict? Did you get a result?'

'Yes. Not perfect, but I think we have enough to use as evidence.'

'Great, see you soon,' Field said.

The atmosphere lifted again, smiles all around.

D.C. Simpson walked in carrying her laptop. 'Sorry about the delay, they had to call in somebody to check the CCTV with me. Seems they are short-staffed like us.'

'What have you got?'

'Exactly as you said, sir. Shona Murdoch arrived at work on the Tuesday night carrying a big re-usable shopping bag. We could see there was a black bin bag in it. We followed her walking toward the A and E department then she walked into one of the rooms on the way. When she came out the shopping bag was empty.'

'Let's see,' John said, trying to hide the excitement in his voice.

Natasha sat the laptop on the desk and the D.I. walked round to watch. They all were quiet as they say exactly what Natasha had described.

'Of course, she will say it's something else in the bag,' John cautioned.

'Yes she will, but it's all stacking up,' the boss said in return.

'Okay you 2, get out and make sure we are ready to confront her after the doctor okays her to see us again.'

The 2 Detective Constables left.

'It's been quite a day already,' Chris said. 'Hamilton

and Murdoch both banged up. Hamilton guilty of drunk driving and Murdoch will be lucky to squirm out of this murder charge. That reminds me,' Field said, and picked up the phone.

'Hi, can you tell me when Fionagh Hamilton will be getting released?' she asked the desk sergeant. She nodded when he told her what he wanted to know. 'Great. Is the doctor here to see Shona Murdoch yet?'

'Brilliant,' she said with a smile before putting the phone down.

'Our friend Miss Hamilton is expected to leave here at 18:00. Plenty time to call Chris Maben, a Scottish Sun reporter I know and tell him something to his advantage. We will see how she likes getting her photograph taken.'

John shook his head. He wouldn't have been so underhand, but he wasn't going to complain about her actions either.'

'The latest on the doctor situation was he is expected in half an hour. I am sure he will say she is fit to be interviewed. Don't you?'

'Yes, she was at it,' John conceded.

INTERVIEW NO. 19
SHONA MURDOCH

Interview with Shona Murdoch. Present are Mrs. Murdoch, her lawyer Ben Dorsey, Detective Inspector Chris Field, Detective Sergeant John Rose and Detective Constable Natasha Simpson. August 11th 18:00.

Rose: I hope you are feeling better Shona. Hopefully this will not take long. After you murdered Rosie Baker you returned home and dressed in ppe before putting Rosie in her bed. That was why there was none of your DNA on her body. Is that correct.

Murdoch: No comment.

Rose: You couldn't risk putting the ppe and the flex, or whatever it was you used to murder Rosie, into domestic rubbish. The best thing you could do was take it to the hospital where it could be incinerated. Is that what you did?

Murdoch: No comment.

Rose: We have some CCTV footage we want to show you.

Natasha Simpson turned the laptop towards Shona and Ben Dorsey. They watched it without saying anything.

Rose: That is you on the film, isn't it?

Murdoch: No comment.

Rose: We have heard from the mobile forensics. Rose Warnock's phone was called from your phone at 07:15 on Monday morning. As you were alone at home you must have made that call. Did you make that call?

Murdoch: No comment.

Rose: You left work early on the Monday morning saying you were ill. You weren't ill, it was because you couldn't contact your husband. You assumed he was with Rosie. Didn't you?

Murdoch: No comment.

Rose: Okay Shona, I think we should end just now, let you rest and think about what we have discussed. However, if you are innocent you should be talking to us. Interview terminated at 18:12.

D.I. FIELDS OFFICE 18:30

'WHAT ELSE do we have?' D.I. Field asked.

'Nothing at the moment. I think we have enough, but Dorsey will say it's all circumstantial. Really it is, but the thing is we know she did it and she knows we know.'

'Do you think she will confess? You really think Dorsey wouldn't advise her to put her hand up for it?'

'I will make a prediction, if she does confess she will claim temporary insanity due to her hormonal condition caused by her pregnancy,' John said.

'All we can do now is wait. Fancy a takeaway from the Bar XX tonight? Last nights was good,' Chris said with a smile.

'To be honest I am still ok from the lunch I had. Anyway, if you want anything from there you can go.'

Chris laughed. John didn't.

INTERVIEW NO.20
SHONA MURDOCH

Interview with Shona Murdoch. Present are Mrs. Murdoch,

her lawyer Ben Dorsey, Detective Inspector Chris Field,

Detective Sergeant John Rose and Detective Constable Alfie

Muir. August 11th 19:30

Dorsey: Shona has asked me to read a prepared statement after which she will answer no comment to all questions after that.

On the 5th of August I called on Rosie Baker and accused her of having an affair with my husband Andy. She laughed at me. Our argument got heated, I called her a slut. She called me a fat bitch. She said she hoped my baby died in the womb. Then she pushed me in the chest. I stumbled back fell to the floor. I felt a pain in my belly. She stood over me laughing. After I got up she laughed at me again. When she turned to walk away she said she wouldn't have an affair with Andy because the one time he screwed her he was crap. I was raging and grabbed the first thing that came to me. It was a small lamp in the hallway, I picked it up and was going to hit her with it. Instead, I wrapped the cable around her neck and pulled it. I didn't realise what I was doing until she was dead.

Mrs. Murdoch said at the time she was ill because of the lack of sleep and because she hadn't been taking her medication for depression. She says because of this she will plead guilty to manslaughter but not murder.

Field: If she is not willing to answer any questions we will end the interview now. Interview terminated at 19:40.

INCIDENT ROOM 19:45

CHRIS FIELD walked into the room with arms raised in triumph. 'People, we have a confession,' she said to much cheering. She walked forward then turned to face John who was walking behind her.

'There he is folks, the legend that is John Rose.'

This got John a round of applause from the whole group. He waved his hands and waited until the applause stopped before addressing them.

'Listen folks, I didn't solve this, the team did. So when you are applauding me you are applauding each other. Well done one and all.'

'Right, John, let's get this written up and sent to the procurator fiscal.'

John followed Chris into her office.

'Right, she can forget about her

manslaughter rubbish, we are going for murder. Pushed her to the ground my arse. She went in there to kill her,' Chris said.

'I agree. Think we will hear back tonight,' John wondered.

'Sure we will. Church told them this is top priority.'

'We sit about and wait then,' John said.

D.I. FIELDS OFFICE 23:15

'ARE YOU sure your phone is working?' John asked.

'I know. The waiting is the worst part. I mean she has confessed, what more do they want.'

The office door suddenly shot open. The imposing figure of Detective Chief Inspector Church stood before them.

'You are both here. Good. My weekend has just been disturbed by my boss. It seems you 2 have schemed to get the reporter who showed you up for the incompetent sods you are, getting fitted up for drink driving.'

Chris and John looked at each other. Talk about fake news. Before they could speak the office phone rang. Chris answered it.

'Okay, thanks for that,' she said.

John couldn't even guess from her reaction whether the prosecution service had okayed the charge or not.

Chris looked Church calmly in the eye. 'Sir, that was

the procurator fiscal's office calling. They have just said we can go ahead and charge Shona Murdoch with the murder of Rosie Baker.'

His look changed from simmering rage to not understanding what she was saying and finished at surprise.

'Really? Shona Murdoch, the neighbour. Are you sure?'

'She confessed, you can't get more than sure than that.'

'Well, well done.'

'Sir,' John spoke, 'if you had spoken to the desk sergeant he would have told you that Miss Hamilton was drunk-driving and had a puncture. It was the breakdown driver that called it in before the traffic boys attended. Nothing to do with us, sir.'

'Oh, right. Well, well done again. Good work,' he said, then left with his tail firmly between his legs.

When they saw he was safely out of the Incident room John and Chris burst into fits of laughter.

'Oh John,' Chris said, 'see what you are going to miss.'

'You know you are right; I will miss this.'

THE END

THE END

Printed in Great Britain
by Amazon